THE
SANDMAN

STEVE HIGGS

Vinci Books

vinci-books.com

Published by Vinci Books Ltd in 2025

1

Copyright © Steve Higgs 2021

The author has asserted their moral right to be identified as the author of this work in accordance with the Copyright, Designs and Patents Act 1988. This work is a work of fiction. Names, characters, places and incidents are the product of the author's imagination or are used fictitiously. Any resemblance to actual persons, living or dead, places and incidents is entirely coincidental.

All rights reserved. No part of this publication may be copied, reproduced, distributed, stored in any retrieval system, or transmitted in any form or by any means, including photocopying, recording, or other electronic or mechanical methods, nor used as a source for any form of machine learning including AI datasets, without the prior written permission of the publisher.

The publisher and the author have made every effort to obtain permissions for any third party material used in this book and to comply with copyright law. Any queries in this respect should be brought to the attention of the publisher and any omissions will be corrected in future editions.

A CIP catalogue record for this book is available from the British Library.

Paperback ISBN: 9781036708672

The EU GPSR authorised representative is Logos Europe, 9 rue Nicolas Poussion, 17000 La Rochelle, France contact@logoseurope.eu

By Steve Higgs

Blue Moon Investigations

Paranormal Nonsense
The Phantom of Barker Mill
Amanda Harper Paranormal Detective
The Klowns of Kent
Dead Pirates of Cawsand
In the Doodoo with Voodoo
The Witches of East Malling
Crop Circles, Cows and Crazy Aliens
Whispers in the Rigging
Paws of the Yeti
Under a Blue Moon
Night Work
Lord Hale's Monster
Herne Bay Howlers
Undead Incorporated
The Ghoul of Christmas Past
The Sandman
Jailhouse Golem
Sparks in the Darkness
Shadow in the Mine
Ghost Writer
Monsters Everywhere

Modern Fairy Tale
No Such Thing as Magic

Albert Smith Culinary Capers

Pork Pie Pandemonium
Bakewell Tart Bludgeoning
Stilton Slaughter
Bedfordshire Clanger Calamity
Death of a Yorkshire Pudding
Cumberland Sausage Shocker
Arbroath Smokie Slaying
Dundee Cake Deception
Lancashire Hotpot Peril
Blackpool Rock Bloodshed
Kent Coast Oyster Obliteration
Eton Mess Massacre
Cornish Pasty Conspiracy
The Gastrothief
Lyme Regis Layover
Majestic Mystery

This book is dedicated to Steve Short, a long-time advocate of my work and dedicated member of my inner circle. He is responsible for the camouflage jackets Basic is now making a fortune with.
Thanks, Steve. Top man.

Missing Team Member

FRIDAY, DECEMBER 23RD 1517HRS

Tempest

Amanda and I were all but running as we left the ward. My clothes were on - having dressed in a world record time – but crazily dishevelled and my hair had to be sticking out at all angles because that was what it always did until I tamed it.

None of these things registered in my head as both Amanda and I started talking.

We were having two different conversations, and neither was with each other. I was on my phone to Big Ben. Amanda was on her phone to Hilary.

Two minutes earlier, Chief Inspector Quinn had left my hospital room after dropping a bombshell about Jane. Jane is the third detective at my firm, Blue Moon Investigations, and she was missing. He didn't say she was missing, that would be poor form for a police officer, a senior one to boot, unless he was already doing something about it, but what he did say was enough for me to believe she was in desperate trouble.

Chief Inspector Quinn revealed that Jane had music playing when her phone was answered but there was no one there to talk to. Anyone else would most likely think that was odd yet dismiss it. Amanda and I knew what it meant, and it sent ice through our veins.

The piece of music was *Mr Sandman* by *The Chordettes*, and it was the signature of a serial killer we had dubbed The Sandman. Jane stole one of his recent victims before he could kill her and got a threat through the mail only days later.

It read: *I'm going to sing you to sleep*, and it came with a copy of the record to remove any ambiguity about the sender's identity.

Ever since, Jane had been working on her caseload while never really taking her eye off her investigation into who the Sandman might be in real life. I had left her to get on with it, never really paying enough attention to how great a threat the psycho posed. There had been no further threats from him, and no messages or signs that Jane was being followed. We also had no client for the case and lots of paying work to keep us busy.

I was going to blame myself if anything happened to her, and since she was most likely the captive of a serial killer already, I had to accept that something already had.

Big Ben's sleepy voice reached my ear. 'Hey, normal sized man, what's happening?' Big Ben is an old buddy from the army. He's six feet seven inches of toned, lean muscle with a face that could sell aftershave. He never misses a chance to be a dick.

I cut through all his nonsense fast. 'Jane's been taken, Ben. It's the Sandman.'

I got a beat of silence before he said, 'Where do you need me?' The tone of his voice and entire attitude had switched in a heartbeat. We were dealing with serious business and he was ready.

He got the short answer. 'The office. Amanda is with me. We are just leaving the hospital to get to Rochester. We need to go over Jane's notes first. She's been trying to work out who this guy is for weeks. It's time to finish her work.'

'Okay.' I could hear movement in the background and a woman's voice. Strike that, I could hear at least two different voices — two women. At least. 'I need a few minutes to organise myself. I'll meet you there.'

With that call complete, I called the next number on my mental list. I have a circle of friends just like anyone else. Unlike most people, mine were all heroes. They chose to involve themselves in my work, coming with me when I needed extra muscle or extra brainpower. It rarely goes well.

I called Jagjit, a man who I met at school on my first day. Our careers diverged when we left school, he went to university and I went off to be a soldier. When I left the army and returned home, he was still there, and we picked up where we left off.

Amanda caught my arm to get my attention as the phone rang in my ear. We were still negotiating our way through the crowded hospital and I looked around expecting to see that she was trying to steer me away from something.

It wasn't that; Amanda had something to tell me and a question to ask. 'Hilary is on his way. His wife is not happy.' When was she ever? 'Do you want me to call your parents?'

My mum and dad are kind of kooky. Dad is retired Royal Navy and is the kind of man who gives his son a stupid middle name because he believes it will help him in life. It didn't. Mum crosses herself thirty times a day, tipples on gin and wine and dreams up ways to annoy my father. She vehemently disapproves of my career as a paranormal investigator – my activities cause at least half of the crossing she does – while dad thinks my job is brilliant and keeps joining in.

He has nearly died while helping like eleven times already. He's probably the reason mum finds the need to tipple.

I pursed my lips and shook my head. I didn't want them dragged into this. It is only a day until Christmas, and they are heading to my sister's place in Hampshire for the big day. We would have enough people to go over the information I expected to find.

Having given Amanda my answer, I continued planning in my head. The exit was ahead but we had to slow down as we reached the press of people in the hospital's reception area.

Jagjit finally answered his phone. 'Tempest, what's up?'

Oh, yeah. I should probably introduce myself. My name is Tempest Michaels. I'm a six-foot, one-hundred-and-ninety-pound former British soldier and current paranormal detective. The current job came about by accident but has stuck because it seems to suit me. I employed Amanda because she asked me to, and I said yes because she is a drop-dead gorgeous blonde and the thing in my pants makes decisions for me all too often.

This story is about me. Kind of.

Unpleasant Sensation

FRIDAY, DECEMBER 23RD 1518HRS

Jane

I awoke with a dry mouth. That was the first thing my brain chose to notice, but it took no more than a heartbeat for it to catch up with some of the more pertinent information. Such as my hands being tied behind my back. A ball of cotton wool filled my mouth, hence the dryness, and the moment I felt it there I began to gag. It was held in place by a rag which was tied tightly around my head.

Forcing myself to calm, I got the gagging under control and ran a mental checklist to see what other problems I might have. I couldn't see anything, but I wasn't blind, I was simply in a room devoid of light. I was lying on a bed. A comfortable bed at that; not that being comfortable was giving me any comfort.

Doing my best to think logically, I worked back through recent events. I'd just arrived home late last night, only leaving Frank's super-creepy house in the countryside once I knew Tempest, Amanda and the others were safe. They'd been tracking a team of ex-special forces guys and it all got a bit tense for a while.

They lost Tempest in the woods and couldn't get hold of him. I stayed with Frank until we heard he'd been found, cold, but unharmed.

So I left Frank's house, driving my car back to Gran's house in Aylesford ... but then what? I had a vague sense of arriving home. Exhausted, starving, and wanting a bath even though it was something like two in the morning, I ...

What did I do? I asked myself the question as I wriggled around and tested my bindings. My ankles were tied too, but not my knees which meant I could shuffle my legs around. The ropes – it felt like rope – around my ankles were tight but had been tied over my boots. I was going to be able to get my feet free if I worked at it.

There was nothing holding me to the bed which meant some more shuffling got my legs around to the edge and I was able to carefully sit up. In the dark, I was fearful I might encounter a low ceiling but found nothing but free air.

Okay, I was sitting up. Now what?

Still dredging my memory, I could not recall getting to my house. Everything went blank when I parked the car.

A sudden burst of light burned my eyes as the lights in the room came on. The walls, floor, and ceiling were all bright white and the lights set into the panels above my head were like those erected in a surgical theatre.

My eyes screwed tight shut to defend themselves, but even through my eyelids it still hurt.

'Ah, I see you are awake,' came a disembodied voice. Like the lights, the suddenness of it startled me, making me jolt. It was coming over a speaker, the voice containing that electronic not-quite-rightness and sounding distant even though it was right in the room.

I looked about but could not see the speaker. Guessing it was plastered into the wall, as they can be, I hopped to my feet and tried to find it.

'I hope you are feeling well,' the voice continued, 'and rested. Though not too rested because you will sleep again soon.'

I froze to the spot, my blood turning to ice because in that instant I knew who I was listening to. The Sandman had me. He threatened to sing me to sleep and now I was his captive.

A chuckle came over the airwaves. 'Did you just work it out, Jane Butterworth? Yes, I can see by your body language. There is no reason for alarm, Jane. Nothing terrible is going to happen to you. I merely wish to sing you to sleep. You probably expect me to harbour a grudge because you stole Karen Gilbert from me, yet I do not. I will find Karen again in time, and she can hear her song then.'

I looked around, trying not to appear frantic even though that was exactly how I felt.

Had I not been gagged I might have thought up a witty repartee or launched a salvo of expletives and threats. Since I could do neither, I focused on what I could do – I listened.

He sounded confident, that was the first thing that stuck in my head. His voice was that of a middle-aged man; someone the wrong side of fifty perhaps. His accent was local and educated, by which I mean he sounded like he had attended a private school and came from money. Kent has a gulf of divide between the multi-millionaires living in huge country houses and the breadline living-wage workers stuffed two families to a tiny house. The two live almost next door to each other in some areas.

There was also something familiar about his voice. My brain insisted I knew who I was listening to or that it was someone I had once met. If that were true, I could not yet connect a face to the voice.

The Sandman continued to prattle on, chatting away happily like we were sharing a conversation over a coffee. 'There is no point in looking for a way out, Jane. I'm afraid escape is quite impossible. You should rejoice though for all your worries are over. All the petty concerns you held for relationships, bills ... the future. All will melt away when I sing you to sleep for the final time.'

I hopped back to the bed but continued to look around the room until I spotted the camera lens. It was tiny - a fraction of an inch, no more. A small fraction at that. He could see me, he could hear me, and he held all the cards.

Well, maybe not quite all. My research led me to be convinced he had only ever killed women. According to everyone, my small frame makes me look scrawny when I am dressed as James. To be fair, I get what they are saying. I weigh not much more than a hundred pounds and I'm nearly six feet tall. However, when I choose to become Jane, the attributes change and suddenly I am thought to be willowy or slender – positives for a woman. Is it any wonder I spend more time as my feminine persona? Getting my voice to sound right took some time, but I was willing to bet the Sandman, whoever he was, had no idea about my true gender.

If I could find a way to use that to my advantage, I would.

Pooling Resources

FRIDAY, DECEMBER 23RD 1519HRS

Tempest

Not paying enough attention to where I was going, I bumped into someone just as the call to Jagjit connected.

I bounced off the hard shoulder that hit my chest and all but fell backward. My phone was jerked from my hand to go skittering across the tiled floor of the hospital's reception area.

Thrusting a leg back to arrest my motion, I turned to see who I had bumped. A man with a buzz cut was glaring at me. He was in his thirties and dressed like a monk. Sort of. His cassock – I believed that was the right word for his thick floor-length robe – was black. A large hood fell behind his head and his sleeves hung low beneath his arms which were tense and ready to rise into a fighting stance.

So, he looked like a monk, sort of, but he clearly wasn't one. The tattoos on his neck and knuckles and a scar on his jawline were other indicators. I couldn't see his feet, but I doubted he was wearing sandals. From the grimace on his face, I thought combat boots were more likely.

'You should watch where you are going, sonny,' he growled.

Honestly, I thought the man I walked into connected with me on purpose, but I had no time for nonsense right now, so he was getting the benefit of the doubt.

'Terribly sorry,' I offered him, making my face as emotionless as possible. 'I was distracted. Are you hurt?'

'Hurt?' he sneered. 'You think you can hurt me?'

I was being challenged, something which would normally be seen as free permission to demonstrate why people ought to not challenge me. This was not the time.

Amanda returned with my phone. 'Everything okay?' she asked.

I was already on edge and very much wanting to find someone to punch – namely the Sandman. Monk-from-Hell would do for now but venting my frustration in public was only going to delay me getting to Jane – hospital security were only yards away.

'It's nothing,' I replied, setting off for the doors again and putting the idiot from my mind.

'Go on. Walk away,' he goaded to my back. 'Next time it won't be an option.'

Amanda sensed me tense and grabbed my arm. 'There's no time,' she reminded me needlessly.

I felt the sense of urgency most keenly. We were likely to pull an all-nighter, refusing to stop our research and investigation until we found a thread to unravel. How could we give up and go to bed when we knew Jane was out there somewhere?

Exiting the hospital, I spotted the chief inspector ahead and started running. He was about to get into his car.

'Yo! Quinn!' I shouted loud enough to make him turn his head. There were other officers around him - his small entourage of butt kissers no doubt.

He didn't bother to wait to see what I wanted. Despite observing me running in his direction, he opted to doff his hat and slide into the passenger seat of a squad car instead.

The car was pulling out of its parking space by the time I got there, the chief inspector pointing for the driver to go around me.

I threw myself on the bonnet of the car. *Try driving now.*

Quinn puffed out his cheeks in annoyance and a small tic appeared by the corner of his left eye. That I was upsetting him bothered me not the slightest.

'Jane Butterworth has been kidnapped by a serial killer!' I shouted through the windscreen.

Reluctantly, he motioned for his driver to switch off the engine and picked up his hat once more.

I waited until he got out of the car before I slid down from the bonnet and back onto my feet. 'That music you hear on her phone, Chief Inspector, surely you recognised it?'

He twitched an eyebrow. 'What of it?'

'The Sandman,' I knew he knew what I was talking of. 'He was responsible for terrorising a woman called Karen Gilbert. That was at the start of this month. There was a fire at her house, and she is still in hiding. Jane's research showed there were other cases going back years. Do you really not have someone looking into it? You were involved in the case,' I pointed out while doing my best to keep my exasperation in check.

He tapped a thoughtful finger to his chin and crossed his arms. 'The Sandman. Yes, I do remember *Mr* Butterworth expressing some concern about it.'

I snapped. 'She saved your life, Ian,' I pointed out, coming forward a foot so I was right in his face. 'She nearly lost hers doing it, and yet you cannot manage to respect her right to determine her own gender.'

There were several things I knew for sure about Chief Inspector Ian Quinn: he hated being addressed by his first name, and he truly hated that his life was saved by a person he privately considered to be a crossdressing freak.

Before he had a chance to retort, I launched my next salvo. 'You have a serial killer operating in the area with murders going back years. If you don't get off your backside and get involved in trying to find Jane Butterworth, so help me when I bust this case open and catch the guy behind it, I will publicly destroy you.'

My teeth were gritted together as we stared menacingly into each other's eyes.

His driver was out of the car, so too a pair of sergeants from the other car. Had they not known who I was, or had former constable, Amanda Harper, not been with me, I think they would have moved to intervene.

They didn't, and Quinn was forced to deal with me. He broke the gaze first, fishing in his pocket for a handkerchief. Using it to wipe his face as if I had covered him in rabid spittle, he said nothing until he was ready.

'The Sandman is a figment of an overactive imagination, Mr Michaels. There is no serial killer operating in Kent and if you tell the press there is, I shall seek to destroy you for inciting panic. *Mr* Butterworth,' my fists clenched, 'is most likely engaged in some strange and sordid sex event. I shall, nevertheless, diligently explore the possibility that something untoward might have befallen *him*.'

There it was. Chief Inspector Quinn would never willingly admit he could be wrong or agree with any course of action I might suggest. However, now that he had stated what a waste of time it was going to be, he was going to rush back to the station and start a full investigation.

Much like Hell Monk – I renamed him in my head - my frustration and anger at Jane's situation were behind my outburst and desire to resort to violence. Hitting Quinn might be one of the most satisfying things I would ever do in my life, but I would hand him the chance to lock me up and that had to be right up there on his top few most desirable things to do.

Letting a slow breath go, I relaxed my posture and brushed an imaginary piece of lint from his left shoulder.

'Claim the collar if you must, Ian. I genuinely don't care. But please put some resources to this case. The clock is ticking, and the sun is beginning to set.'

It was already getting dark.

He narrowed his eyes at me. 'You don't get to tell me my job, Mr Michaels.' He stepped away, grabbing the handle of his car to open it but pausing to deliver one last line before he did. 'If you ever touch me again, I'll arrest you. Is that clear?'

He expected me to say, 'Crystal,' or something like that. Instead, I hit him with a smile and walked away. We needed to get to the office and fast, but I had one last thing to say. Calling over my shoulder, I told him, 'I'll send you a copy of our file. Everything you need will be in it.'

If he had a response for me, he chose to keep it to himself. The sound of the squad car doors closing was followed a moment later by their engines starting.

'Where's your car?' I asked Amanda, scanning around for her Mini.

She chuckled. 'It got blown up yesterday, remember?'

I had, in fact, forgotten that inconvenient truth. Her

beloved Mini Cooper burst into a ball of flame that was intended to kill the pair of us. It happened right outside Maidstone Police station as a demonstration of confidence by the men we were after. They thought themselves to be untouchable ghosts, but ultimately that was their undoing.

'So what are you driving?' I wanted to know.

I got a wide and sexy grin in reply. 'That.' She pointed.

How I hadn't spotted it when it was not only the sexiest car in sight but was also mine, defied belief. The sleek, white series 1 Lotus Esprit was a gift I received the previous day. Or was it the day before? The last few were nothing but a blur as days merged into nights and I got altogether far too little sleep.

Had it not been for my brush with hypothermia and subsequent hospital stay, my tank would be close to empty right now. As it was, I had slept for a good chunk of the day, obeying the doctors because I knew I ought to.

'I pinched it earlier so I could collect you. I hope you don't mind,' Amanda knew I wouldn't but was being polite anyway. Not waiting for me to answer, she said, 'It is sooo much fun to drive, by the way. And fast. My goodness, you hit the accelerator in this, and it tries to leap off the side of the planet.'

My girlfriend/business partner was gushing with excitement, her face flushed with the memory of driving the low-slung, vintage British sports car.

With a smile that felt out of place given what we needed to do, I said, 'Well, we are in a hurry. Why don't you show me?'

First Steps

FRIDAY, DECEMBER 23RD 1554HRS

Jane

The Sandman prattled on for what felt like an age but was probably only fifteen minutes. I wasn't offering much by way of conversation, of course. He excused himself ever so politely when he needed to end our little chat, as he put it; he had other matters to which he felt he must attend.

He did not specify what those matters might be.

I'd been stripped of my possessions, my handbag with phone and other items I might be able to use was somewhere I was not. It could be in my car still for all I knew. The point is that it wasn't with me so all I had to work with were the items in the room.

There were no windows, and the door was electronically sealed I assumed since it didn't have a handle. The only item of furniture in the room was a single bed. The mattress was made from memory foam and the bed was bolted to the floor. The walls were smooth; one might even call them faultless, and there was no light switch.

Wherever I was, it was a place designed to hold people captive and give them no hope. I wanted to curl into a ball and weep. I almost did, but rolling back onto the bed and feeling sorry for myself, I knew I was choosing to accept my fate.

And I did not accept it.

For three weeks, I had been trying to figure out who this guy was, but he just didn't leave any clues behind. There was no way of even knowing how many victims there might be. Any woman who went missing could be one of them.

The woman who led me to the case, Karen Gilbert, said there was no sign of forced entry to her house - the Sandman just let himself in. That meant he had a key. I asked her to name all the people who had keys, but it was a pool of one: her parents.

The Sandman had a specific method of operation. In each case, he would select his victim and break into their house multiple times to sing to them in their sleep. He induced an alert yet immobile state – I still wasn't sure how – so his victims could do nothing about their predicament. Once he'd toyed with them for long enough, he kidnapped and killed them. Or, at least, that was my best guess. Like I said, he left very few clues.

After three weeks of patient research in between my other cases, I still hadn't found any more victims I could be certain were his. I found one early on by the name of River Tam. She was found in a field, posed as if sleeping with a pillow and blanket. She'd reported dreaming about the Sandman on a website for insomniacs which was how I could be fairly certain she was one of his, and it was her face that took me a stage further.

She resembled Karen Gilbert so closely the two could be sisters. When I started looking for other women with the same features, who were roughly the same age, and were also missing, I found a trail going back three decades.

It was chilling and I had little doubt I was going to be right about a great number of them because he wasted no time in threatening to sing me to sleep as well. The way he had just spoken to me made it sound like he believed he was doing his victims a favour.

With no clock and no sun, I had no idea what time it might be or how long I had been unconscious before I woke up here. I wasn't tired. In fact, I would go so far as to say I felt refreshed. Given how tired I had been before, did that mean I had been asleep for hours? I was certain I'd been grabbed in the middle of the night. Was it afternoon now?

These were good questions, but not ones that were going to get me free. The first thing I wanted to do was lose the gag. Maybe doing so would cause my kidnapper to come to the room. The thought was terrifying, but I also recognised that I needed him to open the door if I was ever going to escape, plus finding out who I was dealing with sounded like a good idea.

Even if it made me want to wet my pants.

The gag felt like it was a piece of rag. I couldn't see it, and with my hands behind my back, I couldn't touch it either. Or could I? I backed against a wall, folding my arms up at the elbows until my hands were between my collar bones. Then I tilted my head back to bring the back of my skull down. After a few deep breaths, I sunk my weight down the wall. I was attempting to force my fingertips upwards to get to the material as it went around the back of my head.

I can report that this is not something that a human can achieve. Not a normal one with bones anyway. I got close, which is say maybe less than two inches away, but close wasn't going to win me any prizes.

Changing tactic, I got onto the floor and pulled my knees up to my face. I had to shuffle a little but found that getting my arms out from behind my back was far easier than I thought it would be.

Now with my arms in front of my body, reaching up to my face to lose the gag was equally easy.

He must have seen me remove my gag. How quickly would he react?

Working my jaw and lips around to loosen them off once I got the awful ball of cotton wool from my mouth, I waited for the sound of feet outside or for his voice to boom over the speaker again.

No footsteps or voice came.

I couldn't decide if that was good or bad.

Listening to my heart pound in my chest, I waited what had to be another minute before I moved again. He was able to see me, and hear me, but only if he was watching. Maybe the other things he needed to do took him away from the screen.

He could be watching TV or doing the ironing. Or sitting with his family for all I knew. Was I in a secret room in his basement and the psycho had a wife and kids who were oblivious to his murderous nature? I could keep on guessing or I could focus my efforts on something constructive, so that was what I did.

My wrists and ankles were bound with rope that had then been wrapped in duct tape. Starting with my wrists and using my teeth, I worked a corner of the tape free and started to unwind it. I could only do so by yanking it with my head. The process soon gave me neck ache, yet I ignored it much as I was certain Tempest would.

I wanted to stop glancing at the tiny camera lens, but it was the only thing in the room worth looking at and it drew my attention. My imagination conjured all manner of images, picturing the Sandman sharpening an evil-looking knife or fiddling with the piece of rope he planned to use to strangle me.

My pulse refused to slow down, and the damned duct tape was getting stuck to my hair. That was a trivial concern, of course, but another one on my list.

Finally, after several minutes of effort that made my teeth hurt even more than my neck, the last of the duct tape came free. Now able to see the rope binding my wrists together, I could see how difficult it was going to be to get free. Wherever the end was, I couldn't see it, so it had to be tucked up inside the layers running around my wrists.

The sandman was good at ropes and knots. Was that a clue?

Accepting that getting my hands free was going to be the toughest challenge, I had another look at my feet.

The Blue Moon Office

FRIDAY, DECEMBER 23RD 1607HRS

Tempest

By the time Amanda parked the car it was fully dark outside, indiscernible from night-time even though people keeping office hours were still at work. Light from Rochester High Street illuminated the buildings, giving them a soft glow that balanced the deliberate lighting thrown upward to highlight the ancient cathedral. Just around the corner, hidden from view was an even older castle. That I had done battle there more than once and emerged victorious each time made it a special place for me.

There were no lights on in our office and no cars parked behind it save for the Lotus now. Amanda killed the ignition, plunging us back into semi-darkness as the car's lights went out.

Getting out of a Lotus Esprit is not for the infirm or frail. Even lower than my Porsche Boxster, the people inside are almost on the ground so getting out with dignity is a skill. I can only imagine how complex it must be in a skirt.

Nevertheless, exhilarated from the ride, we clambered out and went into our building.

The lights of the office were still blinking on when Big Ben arrived. He was not alone.

'I stopped off in Finchampstead to collect Basic and Hilary,' he explained as the two men filed into the main office space behind him.

I gave them both a wave of greeting accompanied by a suitably grim smile. 'Thanks for coming, guys. I hope I wasn't interrupting anything.'

Amanda was flicking on the various computers around the office. There were tower PCs in my office and hers plus another on the front desk where Jane still worked most of the time. Originally hired as my assistant, she soon proved to be far more capable. We needed to hire a new receptionist person to perform some of the administrative tasks, but that was a long way from the top of the list on a good day – which this wasn't.

The three of us carried laptops most places because our work went home with us – it was just that kind of job, but neither Amanda nor I had ours with us now and Jane's was probably wherever she was.

I walked over to the coffee machine, crab-walking sideways so I could listen to Hilary.

'Basic and I were working on his latest product. It's already proving to be a cash cow.'

Big Ben asked the question first. 'Oh, yeah? What is it?'

Hilary nudged Basic with an elbow. 'Show 'em, genius.'

Here's the thing about James Burham. We call him Basic because he came loaded with only the most basic programming. He can dress himself and feed himself and he held a job for many years parking trolleys at a local supermarket. Beyond that, most concepts escape his ability to grasp, but if you think I am making this sound like an affliction or a disability, you could not be more wrong.

It is a gift.

To start with, the man is perpetually happy. Nothing comes along to ruin his mood, and he is entertained by the simplest things. Second, his lack of intelligence gave rise to marketing ideas no one else in the world could ever dream up.

Recently, he quit his job at the supermarket to pursue a career as an internet entrepreneur. He started by selling air guitars. Yes, that's right, people were paying him for fresh air. They could even pay extra for a signed limited edition. Not long after this took off, he diversified into selling wicked air and radical skids which he performed on his old BMX. His only overhead was the tyres he kept destroying.

I stopped what I was doing to hear what his latest idea might be.

From inside his winter coat, Basic produced a coat hanger. It was a blue plastic one. He held it in the air, looped over the index finger of his right hand. He had a broad, dopey grin on his face.

'It's a coat hanger,' Amanda pointed out.

'S'not,' argued Basic, his grin widening just a little further.

Big Ben bit. 'Okay, what is it then?'

Hilary was struggling to keep his mirth inside.

Basic waved his left hand through the air as if drawing the attention of a crowd to what he held in front of his body.

'It's a camouflage jacket,' he announced.

I blinked.

Amanda turned her head my way, an uncertain expression on her face.

I was trying to fight the laughter, but it forced its way out. Big Ben started howling and soon the five of us were all falling about.

When I could form a sentence, I asked, 'How many have you sold?'

Hilary, Basic's business partner and the one converting the insane ideas into real money, wiped his eyes. 'Twenty-five thousand.' My jaw dropped open. 'In a week,' he added.

It was enough to silence the room. I really wanted to ask how much they were selling them for, but that would be vulgar, so I let it go and got on with making coffee.

Sensing the shift from humour to the deadly business for which we were assembling, Big Ben asked, 'What do you need us to do?'

From her office, Amanda wheeled a large whiteboard on an easel. The pair of us found it easier to visualise the clues in our cases sometimes. Names and places could be quickly jotted with lines connecting them.

As she approached, I started talking.

'At this point, all we know is that a person we suspect to be guilty of killing several women has taken Jane.'

Big Ben shrugged. 'So all she needs to do is fish out the ol' meat and two veg and Robert is your father's brother.'

It had crossed my mind that discovering Jane to really be a man dressed as a woman might ruin the Sandman's plans. However, I doubted the killer's first reaction would be to shake Jane's hand and let her go.

When I expressed that, Big Ben asked, 'You have a plan though, right?'

'Not a plan, exactly. I have a list of things to do and the fervent hope we can work out something from Jane's notes and what we already know. Which isn't a lot,' I added.

'We need to check on Jane's grandmother,' said Amanda, writing *Grandmother* on the whiteboard in big letters.

Big Ben started for the back of the office and the car park beyond. 'Text me an address, I'll see what the old lady knows.'

'Take Basic with you,' I called out. 'He'll be bored here.' Basic jogged to catch up.

Big Ben didn't break his stride. 'Sure thing.'

'And see if Jane's car is there,' I yelled just as the door swung shut.

Big Ben's hand came back through the gap, a thumbs up gesture showing me that he heard.

Then he was gone.

Crossing to the board, I picked up a spare pen to write *Jane's car* in big letters. If we could find it, the location it was in might give us a clue about where she had been taken. Or it might tell us nothing and lead us after a red herring. We wouldn't know until we found it.

Blowing out a breath to steady myself, I was just about to start discussing tasks when someone knocked on the office front door.

Peering to see who it was, I spotted Alice and Jagjit outside looking in.

'I'll get it,' volunteered Hilary, no doubt feeling like a fifth wheel. Our friends came in, adding two more to our number. How many we might need could be debated forever, but I wanted more yet and their arrival had prompted me to consider someone else.

'Does anyone have the number for Jane's boyfriend?' I asked.

Jagjit and Alice knew Jane was missing, presumed kidnapped, because Amanda told them as much on the phone. However, they were in the dark about the Sandman, as was Hilary. I would fill them in as best I could as we went along.

Alice frowned. 'I thought Jane broke up with her boyfriend?' she questioned.

'Jane started dating a cop,' I let her know. 'She met him when we were all in France with the Yeti.'

That appeared to satisfy her thirst for knowledge but if she wanted to know more, Amanda cut her off. 'I know Jan. I'll call one of the girls at the station and get his number.'

'Jan and Jane?' questioned Jagjit. 'That must get confusing.' Putting the matter to one side, he asked the same question Big Ben posed, 'What can we do?'

It was reassuring to have so many good people I could call on at such short notice. Between us, we were going to sift the clues and find Jane. If only I felt as confident as the voice in my head sounded.

Mentioning Jan reminded me to send Quinn Jane's file. Yes, it felt like I was aiding my enemy in a way. The information sharing would never be reciprocated, yet I told myself the chief inspector was not my enemy, he was a tool to be used. My goal was to get Jane back and capture the Sandman. To do that, I should employ every tool I could access.

I sent the email, with almost no text. Just the attached file, and a simple instruction: Read the file, catch a serial killer.

Amanda ended a swift phone call, pulled the phone away from her ear, and focused on the device in her hands still, she said, 'I've got his number. I'll call it now.'

We waited silently, listening to see if her call went through. Quinn might not be on our side but having a serving officer to assist us would be a big boost if Amanda could contact Jan.

She showed us a frustrated face. 'No answer. I'll leave a voicemail and send him a text.' When that was done, she suggested, 'How about Alice, Jagjit, and I go through Jane's notes in my office.' Looking at me she said, 'You and Hilary can work on the same notes out here and we see what we come up with. I haven't looked at her file on the Sandman yet, but since it's Jane it is bound to be extensive. It's going to take all of us to go through it if we want to do it fast.'

Fast was necessary.

We broke into two groups, each heading in a different direction. The coffee machine pinged to let me know it was ready for use, but it got ignored as I slotted into the chair at the reception desk.

Finding the right file was easy enough; we all obeyed a file naming system to make it easy for each other and they all sat on a central server. The file was huge, just as Amanda predicted. It contained photographs, maps, newspaper articles, and statements from relatives. How Jane found all the information was testament to her ability as a researcher.

Plus, she was invested in identifying the person behind the mystery – he was threatening her life too.

'How long have we got?' Hilary asked nervously.

I huffed out a hard breath through my nose. 'I don't know. Not long probably. My guess is that once he takes his victims, the Sandman kills them the same night, but talking to Jane about it, he messes with them for days or weeks before he gets to the point where he performs the kidnap.'

Hilary sounded incredulous when he asked, 'Why?'

I could only shrug. 'Why do any of it? The Sandman is crazy. He breaks into people's homes, sings to them, and then murders them. I think the why of it is irrelevant. The point is, someone has to stop him, the police don't even know he exists, so right now that someone is us.'

'Karen Gilbert,' shouted Alice from Amanda's office. Hilary and I looked up to find her hanging in the doorway. 'Do you have a number for her?'

I knew who Karen was – the woman Jane saved from the Sandman.

I had to shake my head. 'I don't. But I know where she is.' I leapt to my feet. 'I had to visit her, remember? She went to stay with friends. I don't have their number or their address, but I remember where their house is and can find it again. What the heck were their names?' I racked my brains, tugging at my hair and demanding it dredge up the information I so desperately needed.

'Is she important?' asked Alice.

I nodded my head, puffing out my cheeks and closing my eyes as I tried to connect the dots. The names of her friends wouldn't come, but even if they did, I might not be able to get a number for them. It was going to be easier to go there.

To answer Alice's question, I said, 'Karen Gilbert saw the Sandman. She knows what he looks like. In the limited window of time we have to find him, we are bound to come up with a few options for who it might be. If she can point the finger at one of them for definite, well ...'

'You need to find Karen Gilbert,' Alice concluded.

Amanda called out, 'There's no number for Karen that I can find in this file.'

Would there be a number on the invoice Jane filed? I spun the chair around and got up, crossing the office to the back room beyond where we kept equipment and hardcopy files. Behind me, Hilary slipped in the chair to carry on looking through Jane's notes.

Passing me, Jagjit went to the board to start adding notes.

I found the file I wanted in the back office, checked the contents, and took it with me. As we close each file, we write a short report about the case, the persons involved, the outcome, etcetera. It was an additional work burden I often questioned the validity of, but this was not the first time one of us wanted to look something up and found the information easily to hand.

It was filed on the computer system too, but this was swifter with everyone already using the electronic database.

Coming back through the main office space with the file open in front of my nose, I glanced up to see Jagjit write a name on the board: River Tam.

Seeing the name jogged my memory and I stopped to stare at the name. 'She's the one victim Jane found that she was certain the Sandman killed.'

Jagjit wrote down the location where she was found. 'It was two years ago. Jane's notes suggest there are many others, but she admits to guessing. She found River Tam talking about being sung to in her sleep on a website for insomniacs.'

'I've got a printout of the whole thread here,' yelled Amanda so we would hear her. 'It sounds exactly like what happened to Karen Gilbert.' I heard her get up and come to the door of her office. 'You should see her and Karen side by side.'

I raised my eyebrows. 'What?'

'They could be twins,' she told me, gesturing with her head for me to see.

Hurrying across the office, Jagjit and Hilary on my heels, I asked, 'Are they?'

Amanda shook her head. 'No. However, if you look at

some of the other victims Jane believes to have identified ... well, see for yourself.'

On the screen of Amanda's monitor was a series of pictures. Each was of a woman while still alive with the exception of River Tam. River had been arranged in death, so she appeared to be sleeping peacefully. That she had been abandoned in a muddy field notwithstanding, there was nothing about her appearance that suggested she was dead.

What drew the eye though, was how similar the women all looked. Their ages ranged from late twenties to early thirties, each had shoulder-length brown hair, and their features were similar too – high cheeks bones and full lips. They were attractive women and every last one of them was missing except River Tam, who we knew to be dead, and Karen Gilbert, who was in hiding after a lucky escape.

Beneath each picture, Jane had noted the date they went missing, their age, and the location where they lived.

'Is there a map showing these?' I asked, my voice a sudden noise in the otherwise silent office.

Amanda leaned forward to click the mouse, bringing a fresh tab up. Efficient as always, Jane had marked each point on an interactive map. Scrolling over the little red dots showed who had gone missing from which location.

Jagjit made an uncomfortable noise as if his stomach were squirming. 'They are all from Kent,' he observed.

I let my eyes flit across the screen, performing a swift count. 'Twenty-seven,' I announced with a grimace.

Amanda straightened up and stood back from the desk. 'That Jane found so far. There could be many more.'

'Or some of these might not be his victims,' added Alice. 'Isn't that right? We don't know for sure.'

'It's moot,' I argued. 'Whether they are or not, the

Sandman has Jane and plans to kill her. We have to work out where he has taken her, or where he will take her, or who he is.'

My words acted like a shock to get people moving again, all five of us going in different directions with different approaches in mind. I was heading back out in the car to visit the house of Karen Gilbert's friends.

Jane's Gran's House in Aylesford

FRIDAY, DECEMBER 23RD 1622HRS

Big Ben

We found Jane's car easily enough; the dark grey Aston Martin Vantage wasn't exactly hard to spot. It was testament to the tranquil, safe setting in which her grandmother lived that Jane's handbag, laptop, and other possessions were still in it even though the car wasn't locked.

'She forgot her things,' said Basic with a grin. He probably hadn't fully grasped that Jane had been kidnapped and was most likely in mortal danger even as we poked about her car.

I took her things, unlocking my car again to place them in the rear footwell behind my seat. There was no sign of a struggle and no sign of her keys. I got into a press up position to check under the car just in case the keys went skittering underneath or Jane, sensing her attacker, threw something under there for us to find.

There was nothing. Dusting my hands off as I got up, a glint in the moonlight drew my eye to exactly what I was looking for. Her keys had fallen and come to rest in the shadow of the tyre of the car next to hers – I'd been looking the wrong way.

I fished them out and locked her car.

There was no obvious sign of a struggle, no tell-tale scuff marks on the ground or drops of blood. We checked a wider swathe of the carpark – the only one in Aylesford – but could find no drag marks where someone might have hauled a limp form, their feet trailing behind to leave me something I could follow.

Given that Jane couldn't weigh more than about a hundred and twenty pounds (if that), I accepted that most men could carry her a fair distance should they need to. The Sandman had incapacitated her, either with a stun gun or perhaps by use of an injection of something. Heck, the guy could have gone old school and used chloroform on a rag for all I knew. Either way, the image in my head was of Jane exiting her car and the Sandman coming from behind.

She most likely never saw him.

Finding nothing of use, I gave up and set off for the address I had for her Gran.

We had to cross a small stream to get there, passing through the rear yards of several premises. One was an accountant, another a printing firm. The carpark was dark, the lights erected to chase away the shadows spaced too sparsely to do much about the encroaching night.

I guess that's why I didn't see them.

As I rounded the rear wall of the accountant's and came into an alleyway between the buildings, I bumped into a man. He must have been moving at speed because he hit me far harder than walking pace would allow.

He bounced off, falling backward and tangling his feet to sprawl on the cobbled street.

'Hey!' growled another voice, his friend standing just a few feet away.

It's a truth about me that I have a naturally aggressive posture. Combined with fast reactions, and a willingness to hit first, my senses switched to fight mode the moment the first man stepped from the dark to collide with me.

It is another truth that men see my size as intimidating and often react by starting a fight to prove to themselves that I am not scary. I know, it's completely illogical. However, it happens a lot and I felt sure these two clowns were going to get in my face until I saw what they were wearing.

Aylesford exists because monks built a monastery there many hundreds of years ago. I got to visit it once on a school trip when I was maybe seven or eight. I don't remember much about it other than it was a gloriously hot day and Emma Rigby took off her dress so she could run around in her knickers. I think they had Thursday printed on them.

Anyway, my point is, both men were wearing monks' robes. There is probably a name for the garment, but I had no idea what it might be.

Basic stepped out from behind the wall to join me just as the first man was rolling over to get his feet back under his body.

'Goodness, I'm sorry,' I apologised, reaching out to give the religious man a hand to get off the cobbles.

He slapped my hand away. Roughly and deliberately as if angry at me. It jarred against my image of how he was supposed to behave.

Taking a step back, I had to reassess what I was seeing. They were in their thirties and carried themselves like thugs. Which is to say, they both looked like they were used to throwing their weight around and probably had weapons tucked away somewhere. Their robes were black, not the usual brown I had seen elsewhere and now that I was scrutinising them, their appearance, their postures, and the way they were looking at me told me they were not part of a religious order at all.

And that made them part of a cult.

I mentally labelled the one I knocked down as Flat Top because he had a hairstyle that should have been left in the nineties. His friend I labelled Smiler because his lips were twisted into a sneer that elegantly showed off several missing or chipped teeth.

If there was any doubt left in my mind as to their intentions, Smiler killed them with his next words.

'You need to watch where you're going, sunshine,' he stepped away from the wall to block my path. 'You need to apologise to my friend.'

I punched him in the face. Three times.

The first rocked his head back and I was coming forward to deliver the next blow with my other hand so it caught the underside of his chin as it presented itself. The third blow required me to take yet another fast step because he was falling backward and away from me.

It was more of a glancing blow than anything else and the whole salvo was only at half pace. I wanted him to go away because I needed to be doing other things not messing around with idiots in the dark.

Flat Top was just getting up as his comrade landed. It would have been simple to swing a haymaker downward to fell him once more, yet I gave him the benefit of the doubt and let him dart backward to get a yard between us.

'I don't want any trouble,' I assured both men. Smiler

was on the ground holding his lips, the pair of them looking at me with wide eyes and surprised looks.

This was the point when they would go for their knives or knuckle dusters if they had them.

'You're gonna pay, man!' insisted Flat Top as he grabbed his friend's robe to help him up. Just as Smiler got back on his feet, I took a menacing step in their direction.

It made them get their feet moving, but they didn't let up on the threats as they ran away.

'You're gonna pay, man. You're all gonna pay!'

I watched them for a second as they pelted down the road, beating a retreat.

'Did that strike you as strange?' I asked Basic.

Basic shrugged. 'S'pose.'

Expecting a more detailed response from Basic would be folly, but I hadn't imagined Smiler saying we were all going to pay.

What did that mean?

Working the Problem

FRIDAY, DECEMBER 23RD 1645HRS

Jane

I used a small piece of the duct tape from my wrists to cover the camera lens in the wall. Something about believing he couldn't see me was reassuring.

My feet were free of the ropes and able to move around, which made me feel as though I had achieved something. It wasn't much, I'll grant you, but at least now I had my feet to kick with.

In the last couple of weeks, ever since I took on the stupid Karen Gilbert case that landed me in this mess, I have been attending a twice weekly martial arts class. I had to change classes after the very first one because one of the instructors made it abundantly clear that he wanted to use me as his personal sex toy.

I hadn't learned a lot in two weeks, obviously, but at the same time, since my knowledge base beforehand was zero, I now felt that I could defend myself or even go on the attack if the chance arose.

I knew how to use my body to get the most energy into a kick, and how to break holds if I was grabbed. Such skills might have been really useful had I been conscious when the Sandman grabbed me. There was no sense in dwelling on that, but I satisfied myself that I would know he was coming next time since he would have to come into the cell to fetch me.

With the tape over the camera lens, he would have no idea I was free and ready for him. At least, that was the best scenario I could hope for, and I was indeed hoping.

There were no sounds filtering down to me from whatever lay outside the four perfectly white walls of my cell and when I put my cheek against them, I felt no vibrations either. It was information, but not exactly useful because I had no clue what it meant. The cell could be soundproofed. Or maybe he lived alone and had gone out after he spoke to me.

There had been no reaction to me attempting to get free of my bindings, so it stood to reason he hadn't observed me doing it. With that in mind, I used my fingers to pull my boots back on. They were white leather, knee high with a low heel – I didn't go for big heels often because they made me too tall. They were not the best shoes for escaping a kidnapper, but they were all I had.

What remained as my next task was the bindings on my wrists. Compared to my ankles, which had been sloppy by comparison, bound as they were on the outside of my boots to give me some wiggle room, these did not look like they wanted to yield.

I still hadn't found an end to pick at, nor anything in the room I could use to scratch or scrape at the rope. I'd already had a go at biting the rope and gnawing on it like a dog might. All I'd succeeded in doing was making the rope pink when my gums started to bleed.

The belt on my coat might have been useful if the buckle was tough enough to dig at the rope with, but it had been taken along with anything else I might have been able to use. For added complexity, my wrists were bound so my hands faced each other, so even if I had my belt buckle, manipulating it into a position where I could then use it on the rope might have proven impossible anyway.

Pushing daft thoughts about items I didn't have at my disposal to one side, I got on the floor to look under the bed. I jolted when the bare skin of my arms met the cold tile, swore at myself for being weak, and wriggled like an inverted snake on my back to get under the mattress.

The bed was the only thing in the room and though I claimed that it was comfortable, it didn't have any covers on it, just a memory foam mattress.

There were no springs supporting the mattress; I knew that already but looked around forlornly for anything I might use to work on the rope.

I almost gave up, but just as I was about to begin shimmying back out, I spotted a burr on one of the legs. It wasn't much, and it was awkward as hell to get to but as I rubbed the rope down the leg, it caught.

Just briefly.

I turned my hands over and saw a small tuft of rope had been lifted. It might take me a week to saw through them like this, but I wasn't going anywhere, and I had nothing better to do.

The House of Matilda Carpenter

FRIDAY, DECEMBER 23RD 1648HRS

Tempest

Hilary opted to come with me on the drive to Chartham Hatch. I still couldn't remember the name of the couple I was going to visit but prayed Karen Gilbert was still living with them. The thing is, I didn't think she was.

That I could not remember the things Jane had told me about this case banged around in my head like a haunting reminder. I knew she had talked about Karen Gilbert in the last week or so, and that I was guilty of only half listening. Admittedly, I had several distractions of my own, but it didn't feel like a justifiable excuse right now.

With a huff, I pressed my accelerator a little harder.

'You're worried about her?' asked Hilary, breaking the silence in the car.

I pursed my lips and grimaced into the darkness ahead. 'I am. I don't see how we can possibly work out who this guy is and find him before he does whatever he has planned.'

Carefully, Hilary asked, 'Have you told the police?'

'I shoved it down Quinn's throat,' I growled. 'He will react, but his focus will be on covering his backside, not saving Jane. He would most likely throw all his officers at it if I could provide him with a reliable location and therein lies the crux of our challenge.'

Hilary added up what he already knew. 'No one knows who the Sandman really is.'

I gritted my teeth. 'No. We'll figure it out, you can bet on that. The question is whether we can do that before he kills Jane.'

I fumbled in my jacket pocket to retrieve my phone without taking my eyes off the road. Tossing it to Hilary, I asked, 'Can you call Amanda and put it on speaker, please?'

He fiddled for a moment with the unfamiliar device, but within seconds, Amanda's voice crackled over the airwaves.

'Tempest? Any luck?'

'Not yet. We are nearly there though. Did Jan call back?'

I got a similar answer to the one I gave her. 'Not yet. I'll try him again, but I already left messages and a voicemail. He finished his shift and went home so I guess he is in the bath with the music loud or something.'

The Friday before Christmas – chances are he and Jane had a table for dinner booked somewhere and plans that were completely scuppered though Jan didn't yet know it. I wanted him on the team.

Amanda asked, 'Hey, I just wondered why you hadn't called in Frank and Poison?'

I considered including them right off the bat when we were still running from the hospital. Frank Decaux is the owner of an occult bookshop just around the corner from my office. He's chosen to involve himself in my adventures many times, usually because he believes in everything paranormal and wants to be there when I meet a real vampire or werewolf. If I made the call, I would find him ready to throw his lot in without even telling him what it was that we were doing. Yet his particular brand of wackiness was one that might not lend itself well to this investigation.

Frank would always choose to believe a supernatural explanation first and my head was filled with visions of him extolling the office with tales of demons who liked to sing to their victims. Or he would claim the Sandman was a land-based siren or come up with something even more daft than I could imagine.

I didn't need the distraction and that was how I explained it to Amanda.

Our call ended as I left the motorway near Canterbury. It was less than two miles to the village of Chartham Hatch which we covered in three minutes.

In the street I remembered visiting once before, it took me a few seconds to work out which house I wanted. I was doing it only from memory of a single visit in the daylight and the Christmas lights dotted about were throwing me.

Mercifully, I got it right and the name of the lady of the house popped into my head just as a shadow behind the door opened it.

'Matilda?' I asked as the door swung wide to reveal her grumpy face.

Now I remembered her. She had a brow-beaten husband who she berated constantly during the few minutes I was in the house last time. I came to visit Karen, but Matilda refused to let me out of her sight.

'What do you want?' she asked, her tone unpleasant.

'Merry Christmas,' I replied studiously, to which I received a sneering expression. 'I need to speak with Karen.'

'Well, she is not here,' Matilda snapped back at me. 'She moved out two days after you were last here.'

I could not say I blamed her, but I needed to speak with Karen Gilbert more than I needed oxygen, so I said, 'It is urgent that I talk to her tonight, Matilda. If you are her friend, you will tell me where she is or give me her number.'

She snorted a laugh. 'No chance.'

Unable to stop myself, I closed the gap between us, fighting my rising anger to keep a face that begged for trust.

'Matilda, the Sandman has taken Jane, the investigator who helped Karen three weeks ago.'

'You mean the crossdresser,' she sneered.

Unwilling to be drawn into an argument, I said, 'Yes, that one. Karen could be next. I need to be able to warn her.'

'Well, you're out of luck,' Matilda told me with a shrug of indifference. 'We had a falling out,' *no surprise there*, 'and she went somewhere else. I don't have her number because she changed her phone. I expect she was trying to stop people like you from contacting her.'

Matilda was beyond belief.

'Didn't you hear me?' I wanted to grab her by her shoulder and give her a good shake. 'Karen could die. I need to find her.' Okay, the truth is that I didn't know if Karen was in any danger at all, but it was also true that once we caught the Sandman – potentially with Karen's help – the need to be in hiding would evaporate and all danger of being murdered in her sleep would pass. Being involved was therefore very much in Karen's interest.

Infuriatingly, Matilda shrugged again. 'I can't give you what I don't have. Now, if you don't mind, I'm watching TV.' She stepped back and closed the door.

It bounced off my foot.

When her angry face reappeared, I handed her my card and begged. 'If anything occurs to you, please call me.'

She kicked at my foot, and I removed it. The door slammed in my face.

Hilary said, 'Goodness. What a cow.'

'Christmas spirit,' I commented flippantly.

We had wasted over half an hour already and now we had to get back to the office.

A Show of Strength

FRIDAY, DECEMBER 23RD 1652HRS

Big Ben

I don't really know Jane/James and haven't shared many conversations with him/her ever. I find the crossdressing thing a little odd but make no comment about it. It's not my place to do so and while he and other men are chasing men, I figure that leaves more ladies on the buffet table for me.

It was enough for me that Tempest chose to trust her/him. Tempest never had a bad word to say about his former assistant. In fact, it was more the case that Jane/James continually impressed my old army colleague. She was part of the team. My team. And that someone had chosen to mess with that team did not sit well with me.

So I was going to find the person behind it all and introduce their teeth to their feet. By which I mean I was going to shove one of the feet into their mouth. The other foot I was going to shove … well, I'm sure you can imagine.

Jane's gran lived in a narrow, terraced house right on Aylesford's main street. If you can call it that. Aylesford is more of a hamlet than a village though when you examine the buildings you can see how many used to be pubs or small shops of some kind. Several hundred years old, the street where we found granny's house was no doubt a hub of commerce once.

With Basic looming on my shoulder – he loomed better than anyone I knew; it was his vacant expression and all-round hugeness that created the effect - I politely knocked on the door.

Standing back, so we wouldn't crowd the old dear when she answered the door, we were forced to wait. A minute ticked by, and getting impatient, I stepped back into the narrow street to look up at the house.

There were lights on inside but otherwise there was no sign of life. It presented me with a dilemma.

Given that Jane's things were all inside her car, I doubted she'd made it to the house, but did that mean the Sandman wouldn't come here? From the little I knew, his normal method of working involved going into people's houses. Had he done something to granny?

Eyeing the front door and biting my lip, I considered kicking it in. I knocked again for good measure and got the same result as before.

Time continued to slip away.

There was no point calling the police – they would take ages to do anything and that was if I were able to convince them to act at all. I didn't live here and could provide no evidence there was anything untoward occurring.

Nodding my head as I accepted the damage I was about to do, I swept my left arm through the air to shift Basic back a couple of feet.

'What yer doin'?' he asked.

'Granny might be hurt, or she might be kidnapped like

Jane. There might be clues inside. There could even be a note from the Sandman for all I know. We can't leave until we know the answers.' Looking at the solid oak door which had probably been inside the frame since the house was erected in the eighteenth century, I reconsidered my plan. Or rather, I upgraded it.

'Go for it, Basic. Knock the door down.' Rather him than me because it looked like it wasn't going to give on the first go.

His forehead shifted slightly, Basic frowning as he processed my instruction.

'Knock it down?' he questioned.

I nodded encouragingly. 'Yup.'

He was about to take a run at it when voices cut through the late afternoon air. I gripped Basic's arm to stop him moving.

To the left of Granny's house is Aylesford's one remaining public house still in business. I couldn't guess how long ago the others shut down, but this one was doing a good trade. It was the Friday before Christmas and no doubt most of the people inside were already finished with work for the holiday.

The voices were coming from the doorway of the pub as a gaggle of ladies left. They were all in their twenties and they were not only attractive but also clearly a few glasses of pinot into their Christmas spirit. The jingle of keys told me one of their number was a designated driver and they would have to walk past us to get to the carpark.

'Best if I tackle this one,' I announced loud enough for them to hear. Then I stripped off my jacket to reveal the tight t-shirt I wore beneath.

You would too if you looked like me. Trust me on this.

Making sure to flex and look dramatic, I paid the young

ladies no attention at all but made it clear I was about to kick my way into the house by calling out, 'Don't worry, Granny. We're coming!'

The ladies were watching me. I didn't have to check to make sure - all women watch me; it's just one of those things I learned to accept a long time ago. They were watching me, and their hearts were going pitter-patter as their eyes picked out the stark outline of muscle moving under the single layer of thin cotton covering my torso.

Having no doubt the door would require extra welly if I were going to burst the lock with one kick, I thrust off in a charge. Three paces later, I swivelled on my left foot, brought my right up and drove it through the door about two inches above the handle.

Except I didn't.

I bounced off and felt like I broke my leg in about eight places.

The door didn't shift so much as a hair's breadth, but I was right that the ladies were watching me.

I could tell by their laughter.

The right thing to do at this juncture was deliver a cool line about them not making doors like that anymore, but I kept my mouth shut for fear I might squeak if I attempted to speak.

Mercifully, the ladies decided they were getting cold watching the muscular buffoon who was now lying on the ground wishing he'd let Basic have first dibs after all.

'Dat didn't work, Ben,' Basic pointed out helpfully.

I staggered back to my feet, still unable to speak.

'I fink ders someone coming,' Basic commented just before the house's outside light came on.

'Won't be a minute, love,' came a wobbly old-lady voice from behind the door.

We could hear someone grunting with something heavy inside. Was there something behind the door?

The familiar sound of a lock tumbling preceded the door opening.

'You're supposed to text when you are on your way, Jane,' wobbled the voice. Then the door opened enough for the lady inside to look out. 'Oh,' she gasped upon seeing Basic looming and me rubbing some life back into my right leg.

Before she could slam the door shut again, I gave her a friendly smile and wave. 'I'm Ben, this is James,' I indicated Basic who did his usual goofy grin that always made him look harmless. 'We're friends of Jane. Can we come in?'

Granny looked rightly uncertain about agreeing to my request. 'She's not here,' Granny told us. 'Maybe you should call her.' Jane's grandmother wore house slippers and a long, thick winter coat which she held closed with one hand at the top rather than do all the buttons up just to answer the door.

Her hair was getting thin and had turned to an almost pure white, but there was plenty of it. Either freshly permed or naturally curly, I suspected the former to be true, it made her head look like a snow-covered novelty microphone.

I wanted to deliver our news and have a chat with Jane's grandmother inside the house, not in the street. Not just because of the cold outside, I had serious concerns about delivering my bad news and what it might do to the old dear's heart.

However, faced with little option, I said, 'Her phone is in her handbag which is in my car. I found it in her car along with her laptop and other things. We believe the Sandman has her.'

The Sandman

The old lady gasped and gripped her coat more tightly to her neck.

'You've heard that name before,' I stated. It was clear from the way she gasped that she understood the significance of my claim.

She took a step back. 'You'd better come in, boys.'

Research at the Office

FRIDAY, DECEMBER 23RD 1652HRS

Amanda

Rightly or wrongly, Jane had not entered any details in the file, hardcopy or electronic, by which we could contact Karen Gilbert. I hoped Tempest would get what he needed from the couple in Chartham Hatch but would try to solve the problem here too if I could.

That Karen, the Sandman's most recent target that we knew of, could provide us with any helpful information was debatable. However, she presented a worthwhile target for our efforts, and we needed to speak to her. If she were able to identify the Sandman from a picture, it might prove pivotal.

I was working in my office using my PC while Alice and Jagjit were next door using the computer in Tempest's office.

I left them to it, compiling a list of likely people who might be able to lead me to Karen's current whereabouts. I had already tried her listed place of work only to discover she quit three weeks ago. I had to feel sorry for the woman. She'd been to the police and reported her nighttime home invader only to have her claims dismissed. As a result, she was in hiding, sleeping on someone's spare bed probably, and had no job.

She had several living relatives including a sister in Dudley. I started there, but the woman I got through to was both evasive and rude. My guess was that Karen had briefed her to not give out any details, so it was no great surprise when the phone went dead in my ear.

Usually, when we have a task like this it falls to Jane. She has a natural skill that allows her to find details via the internet the rest of us might never uncover. I knew she used social media to track people down a lot of the time. Once inside someone's personal account it is simple to look at pictures and pick out the people who appear most. If you take lots of pictures of someone and display them, it's likely they are close to you. Armed with that knowledge, she could begin to pick apart their lives.

Unfortunately, I had no idea how to hack my way into someone's social media account.

'Amanda?' Alice's voice floated through the air.

I got up and wandered around to Tempest's office on the other side of the wall to mine.

Jagjit and Alice were sitting shoulder to shoulder, both transfixed by whatever was on the screen to their front.

'Found something?' I asked hopefully.

Their eyes never left the screen. 'Maybe,' Alice murmured. 'A clue, perhaps.' I was all ears. 'Jane recorded that the Sandman was able to get into Karen's home despite it being locked. There was no damage done so he had to have a key, right?'

It was a logical conclusion, and I didn't wish to derail her train of thought so I said, 'Could be a relative?'

She tore her eyes away from the screen to look at me. 'That was my immediate thought, but if we believe him to be responsible for killing dozens of women, he cannot be a relative to all of them. Who else do people give keys to?'

I saw it instantly. 'Neighbours.'

Alice continued. 'I bet Karen had someone she was friendly with. Someone must have had a key, but even if she didn't give them one, it could have been the previous owners who gave a key away. How many people change the locks when they move in?'

Her argument was logical, but I could see a major flaw. 'You said the Sandman couldn't be a relative to all his victims. Surely, he wasn't a neighbour to them all either.'

Seeing my point, she grimaced. 'I should have thought of that.'

Not to discourage her, I said, 'This is good. We are spit balling different ideas. One of them will pay off and lead us to the next logical step. Maybe there is something in this after all. I'm going to speak with Tempest and see if he wants to do a drive by Karen's house. He can speak to the neighbours and see what he digs up. One of them might have a forwarding address for her mail.'

Alice turned her attention back to the computer screen. 'Wish him luck from me.'

Luck. We were going to need it.

Inside Grandma's House

FRIDAY, DECEMBER 23RD 1653HRS

Big Ben

Coming into Jane's gran's house, I let the old lady know our names. 'I'm Benjamin. I work with Jane and the others sometimes when they want a hand with something. This is James,' I indicated Basic and gave her his real name rather than confuse things with an explanation.

Basic said, 'Hullo, Jane's gran.'

Granny frowned as if deep in thought and wriggled her top dentures from left to right. 'That would make you Big Ben and Basic, yes?'

Surprised, I could only nod and chuckle. 'Guilty,' I admitted.

'Jane talks about her work a lot,' granny explained. 'She says you're a bit of a dick.'

A snort of laughter escaped me. 'Guilty,' I said again.

Now inside the small living room, I could see why I hadn't been able to break down the door. Either side of the door frame were two steel brackets. Mounted to the wall, they were a U shape. Their appearance and purpose might have been confusing were it not for the large oak beam leaning against the wall.

'Can you give me a hand to get this back in place, dearies?' asked Jane's gran. 'It's ever so heavy.'

It wasn't. I picked it up with one hand, but though I didn't struggle to lift it, I had to acknowledge that it was solid. I slotted it back into place where it formed a barrier behind the door. Held in place by the brackets, no one was ever getting into the house without a battering ram.

I felt a little better about failing to even make the door rattle when I kicked it.

'Did Jane fit this?' I asked, examining the brackets. There were tiny traces of brick dust on the carpet where the vacuum cleaner had failed to get them, a sure indication that someone had been drilling holes recently.

Gran nodded. 'There's another one on the back door. Jane said we needed a countermeasure because the Sandman was able to open doors even when they were locked. Is he magic?' she asked.

I raised an eyebrow. 'Magic? No, I don't think so. A locksmith maybe but not magic.'

A locksmith?

I'd said it as a throwaway comment, but now I found myself questioning if maybe that thought held some merit. How many of the victims reported no damage to their locks and doors when they were visited? I had no idea what the answer to that might be, but my impression was that we didn't know much about the other victims at all. What I did know, from a chance conversation with Tempest, was that the victim who came to us reported her doors were locked when she was visited.

'When did you last hear from Jane?' I asked, as Jane's

gran led us deeper into the house. The building had oak beams running along the ceiling, and built several centuries ago, it was not intended to accommodate people of my height. Even standing between the beams, I had to tilt my head to the side to make it fit.

Gran shuffled through a door and past the foot of the stairs to access the back of the house. There would be a small kitchen and dining room there.

She called over her shoulder. 'I was just making a cup of tea, boys. Would you like one?'

I could think of no reason not to. 'That sounds lovely. We really need to know about Jane though,' I prompted her.

'Yes, dear. You asked when I last heard from her. That would be yesterday. She doesn't come home every day. Sometimes she stays at her boyfriend's place; he lives in Maidstone. Jan his name is. I think it's spelled with a J but pronounced Yan. Odd foreign name. He's a police officer. I was always quite partial to a man in uniform myself.'

She was wandering off topic again. I did my best to keep her mind on the subject.

'Did Jane mention ever that she saw someone watching her? Did anyone ever try to get into the house?'

'Oh, no, nothing like that.' Gran poured the tea from a teapot that wore a knitted cozy in the shape of a pig. The spout came out of its snout. She used delicate China cups and saucers, the type where one must raise one's pinky when drinking. The tiny handles were far too small for either Basic or me to get a finger through. She set the cups around a small round dining table I could barely get my legs under. Basic's chair creaked and groaned worryingly when he sat on it.

'Have you noticed anyone watching the house? Or seen

a person in the street more than once in a day? Someone who isn't a neighbour,' I clarified.

Jane's gran was diligent in racking her brains to come up with an answer, but it was still a solid no.

'Do you think this Sandman has her then?' gran wanted to know.

I didn't like that I had to answer that question. However, I went with the truth.

'I suspect that to be the case, yes.' Tempest is convinced, which would be good enough for me normally. Having found Jane's car with all her things abandoned in it, any residual doubt had been swept away.

'Oh, dear.' Jane's gran took a sip of her tea,

Seeing the worry etched into gran's face I felt a need to reassure her. 'We are trying to find her, and I can promise you we are pooling all our resources to achieve that. Can I see her room, please? I want to see if she has any notes there that the team don't know about.'

'Of course, dear.' Gran pushed herself back out of her chair. 'I'll show you where it is.'

Muscular Overload

FRIDAY DECEMBER 23RD 1701HRS

Jane

My arms, particularly my shoulders, were aching to the point that the pain in my joints was becoming a burning sensation. My abs hurt too as I had to crunch them to hold my upper body off the floor enough to move my arms.

Every minute or so I would take a break. I had to. The rope was fraying, but it was doing so at a glacial pace. It was the case that I believed cutting through the rope required only my persistence, but though I tried to focus on that thought, a miserable voice inside my head kept reminding me I had no idea how long it would take and that once my hands were free, I still had the challenge of getting out of the room.

However, I was also certain that the Sandman intended to kill me so doing what I could to avoid that fate felt necessary. If nothing else, having my hands free would make fighting easier and I was already resigned to the probability that I would not get away without facing him.

The thought terrified me. I still didn't know what he looked like. He could be a hulking bear of a man like Big Ben for all I knew. How would I beat someone like that?

Gritting my teeth against the pain in my shoulders, I continued to scratch the rope against the tiny burr of steel.

Jane's Bedroom

FRIDAY, DECEMBER 23RD 1709HRS

Big Ben

Jane's room looked just how I imagine a teenage girl's would look. I need to be clear that I have not been in a teenage girl's bedroom since I was also a teenager. Anyway, there was a lot of *Hello Kitty* merchandise, fluffy plush toys, and an abundance of pink. In stark contrast to all the girly stuff was a stack of books on her bedside table.

They were all about serial killers: their psychology, motivations, and behaviour. I tilted my head to read a few titles. Most of them were case studies.

I couldn't help but get the impression she was trying too hard to compensate for the penis in her knickers. I didn't say that though because granny was standing two feet away.

Jane's room also had a lot of notes stuck to one of the walls. Some were coloured sticky squares and others were photographs or newspaper clippings. I pulled out my phone to take some pictures.

There were no notebooks but there was an old vinyl

record. I picked it up for a better look even though I felt sure I already knew what it was.

Basic, usually silent, spoke for once. 'Ders no record player.'

He was correct. Jane had a wireless speaker sitting on a shelf ready to receive instruction from her phone or other device. I doubted Jane wanted to play this song though, given what it represented.

I placed the copy of *Mr Sandman* back where it had been and continued to look around.

'What are you hoping to find?' asked Jane's gran.

I huffed a breath through my nose. 'A big fat clue would be nice.' The truth is that I didn't know what I was looking for. I leave the detective stuff to Tempest. I'm available when someone needs to be punched in the mouth or if there are ladies in need of distraction.

I had photographs of the things on the wall but if there was anything else here worth finding, it would require a different set of eyes. Chances were the good information would be on Jane's laptop and that thought prompted me to get back to the office.

'We're going to go now,' I announced turning around to face the door. 'The rest of the team are working on identifying who the Sandman is. Did Jane ever discuss that with you? Did she ever come up with a hypothesis for who it could be?'

It felt like a long shot, but also entirely possible that Jane would chat about such things with her gran while they ate their dinner or did the washing up.

'No, love, sorry. She did talk about it, but that was because the case was frustrating her. She said it had to be an older person.' Granny's eyes rolled up toward her skull as she dredged her brain for more information but came up blank. 'I think she believed he was someone who avoided social media and was probably killing the women because of something that happened to him many years ago, something traumatic. She could only guess what that might have been, but those books she was reading all pointed to him recreating the act or trying to compensate for what happened.

Gran backed away from the door so Basic and I could leave, but as she started back along the corridor, she paused, remembering something.

'Jane gave me a number to call. She said if anything happened to her, I should make sure someone called this number. Now where did I put that?'

My eyes flared. Would this be something of use?

Following her as she went back to the stairs and started down them, I asked, 'Do you remember who the number was for?'

'Hmmm? Oh, yes. It was Karen something or other.'

Karen Gilbert's House

FRIDAY, DECEMBER 23RD 1730HRS

Tempest

A call from Amanda diverted my return to the office and sent me shooting past Rochester on a northward trajectory. I hadn't been to Karen Gilbert's burned-out house in New Ash Green but though I had no idea where it was, Amanda was able to give me the address from Jane's file and Hilary used the satellite navigation on his phone to get us there.

I pulled up outside the house and shot my cuff to check the time. The street was alight with Christmas. At least fifty percent of the homes were bedecked with lights outside. There were fancy ornaments, lights in trees, lights on roofs. Even the more modestly decorated houses bore lights in their windows where the Christmas tree filled the gap between the curtains.

I found myself filled with a desire to be tucked up in my own place. It was sort of decorated, the lack of effort attributable to how hectic the last few weeks had been. I could be snuggled on the couch with Amanda and the dogs, watching an old movie while ingesting unnecessary calories.

It sounded heavenly, but out of reach until we found Jane. Remembering the man sitting to my left in the Lotus's passenger seat, I said, 'You ought to be at home with your kids.'

He didn't argue, but said, 'What we want isn't always possible. Nor is it always the right thing to do.'

I had to agree with him. Opening my door, I said, 'Let's get this done.'

In horrible contrast to all the other homes in sight, Karen Gilbert's house was covered in a tarpaulin where the fire had eaten away part of the roof. No work had started by the look of it, the house abandoned as she fled to get away from the serial killer stalking her.

No doubt she was having great fun going through the process of claiming on her insurance policy to get the house repaired, but even once liveable, I doubted she would want to move back home unless the Sandman was caught.

That was my job. Self-appointed, but my job, nevertheless.

Out of the car, I looked to my left and right and picked a house at random. Her neighbours might know something, but I doubted it. I was here to get a feel for the case as much as anything else. Jane's investigation was never completed, the client dropping us when she ran away. In hindsight, I should have teamed up with Jane to tackle this sooner. Something else always got in the way though. There was the werewolf case, and then the crazy ex-soldiers.

The Sandman slipped down my priority list and this is where my lack of vision landed us.

I knocked on the door of Karen's neighbour to the left and stood back to wait. A light came on moments later, illuminating the hallway behind the front door and it opened to reveal a woman in her early thirties. She had a baby hooked under one arm and bags under her eyes. She glanced at me, then beyond me to Hilary, who gave her a wave and made a face at the baby, and then back to me.

'Terribly sorry to bother you,' I started. 'I'm not selling anything. I'm helping your neighbour, Karen. Can I beg a few moments of your time?'

The neighbour's name was Katrina Farthing. She remembered Karen and the night of the fire vividly. Karen had been her neighbour since Katrina moved in two years ago, but they never exchanged more than a few words to be sociable when they passed each other. Katrina could not comment on Karen's social life — boyfriends, friends, anything that might have been of use in fact, and she had no idea what might be happening to her neighbour's mail.

My hope that I might uncover something bore no fruit and after a couple of minutes it became clear the lady just wanted to close her door and go back to whatever she had been doing.

'One last question,' I begged. 'I believe Karen has a cat. Do you know who looked after it for her if she ever went away or couldn't get home at the end of the day?'

Finally, I asked a question she could answer. 'That would be Mr Hengist on the other side of her house.'

Hengist. I'd seen the name in Jane's notes earlier. I thanked the young mum and wished her a merry Christmas as she closed the door.

Hilary and I jogged to the neighbour's house on the other side, closing Katrina's gate and opening that of Mr Hengist while being swift about it because time continued to dwindle.

There were lights on in the house, and around the edge

of the curtain in the main bow window next to the front door, came the flickering motion one gets from the TV.

The door swung inward mere moments after I knocked, the person the other side yanking it wide in a rush of sudden movement.

The man on the other side was somewhere around sixty and about five feet nine inches tall. He wore a suit, as if just in from work but not a sharp one that a lawyer or a business leader might wear; his looked a decade old and was being worn because work policy dictated he do so.

His hair was thinning and was cut down to bristles so the stubble on his chin was the same length as that on his head. It was a forgettable face. There was a ring on his finger but no sense from the décor inside that he lived with a woman.

Curiously, his eyes were bugging from his head to make him look panicked and for a moment I thought he was going to slam the door.

To calm his nerves, regardless of what might have given them rise, I gave him the same welcome smile I offered Katrina.

'Hello, my name is,'

'Tempest Michaels,' the man provided, effectively halting me mid-sentence.

'Um, yes,' I agreed, a little off-balance. 'This is my associate, Brian Clinton.' I indicated the form standing in my shadow.

'Sorry,' the man's face became a smile, and he thrust out his hand. 'I recognize you from the papers, that's all. I'm Harry. Harry Hengist.' He was still holding my hand but let it go now that he had said his name. 'I have ... I guess you could call it an amateur interest in the paranormal. I have had for years. It's all so fascinating and enticing to believe there are devious and magical creatures living amongst us. I'm going to guess you are here to follow up on that thing with my neighbour a few weeks ago. Terrible business.'

'That's right,' I agreed again. That he knew who I was and what I wanted was going to speed things up. 'I'm hoping to ask a few questions.'

'Of course,' he encouraged. 'Fire away. I take it that blonde woman was one of your investigators.'

'Blonde woman?' I questioned before realising he meant Jane. 'Oh, yes. That's Jane Butterworth. I'm picking up where she left off.'

'Saucy little thing she is,' the man commented unnecessarily. 'I normally go for brunettes, but there was something about her, you know. Did she tell you she tackled me and pinned me to the carpet?'

I had been about to fire a question at him in a bid to alter the course of the conversation away from Jane and her sauciness, but I needed to hear about her getting physical with Karen's neighbour.

Frowning with my surprise, I said, 'No. How did that come to happen?'

Mr Hengist chuckled. 'I was in Karen's house – she had a parcel come to my place by mistake and I helped her carry it in. Jane saw me, didn't know who I was, and the next thing I knew, I was getting friendly with the carpet.' He laughed at his own choice of phrase.

I would ask Jane about it when I had the chance to, but it wasn't pertinent right now.

'Mr Hengist,' I started.

'Harry,' he cut over the top of me to insist.

I carried on regardless, 'I need to track Karen down, has she given you a forwarding address for her mail or any way to contact her?'

I got an apologetic face in response. 'No, sorry. Nothing like that. We were just neighbours. I don't know what she is doing about her mail.'

'Do you have a spare key to her house?' I had to raise a hand to reassure him when I saw the change in expression. 'I'm not here to accuse anyone of anything. I'm just trying to establish a few base facts.'

He shook his head. 'I don't have a key. Maybe one of the other people here does. Have you tried Katrina on the other side?'

I didn't answer his question. 'At the time of Jane's investigation and the fire that broke out, did you see anyone new in the street? Is there anyone who has moved in recently or anyone you ever saw outside Karen's house?'

Again, Harry shook his head. 'No. I wish I could help you. This is a quiet neighbourhood. Nothing ever happens here. I don't even remember the last time I heard about a burglary. I knew nothing about Karen's situation either. I take it the Sandman is still at large?'

I reacted instantly, the signal reaching my muscles and telling them to move without my brain getting involved at any point. In a flash, I was inside his house and had Mr Hengist pinned to the wall.

'How do you know about the Sandman?' I raged in his face. The suspicion that Karen's attacker had to be someone close to her, either in her life or geographically had remained with me. Now I had the creepy guy next door talking about the Sandman when I was damned certain Karen wouldn't have told him about it. How did he know it? It certainly hadn't been in the papers.

Struggling for breath as my right forearm pressed against his throat, he wanted to say something, but I wasn't waiting for him to get his wits back.

A swift leg sweep took him from vertical to horizontal, my arms steering his torso so that he landed face down with his right arm twisted behind his back.

Hilary gasped and loomed in the open doorway as it spilled cold December air into the house.

'Where is Jane?' I demanded. 'What have you done with her? Is she here in this house?' I was looking along the corridor, wondering if this type of house had a basement. I didn't think so but there could be a shed in the garden, or maybe she wasn't here at all and he had her stashed somewhere else.

'Can't breathe,' Harry rasped, my knee on his lower back keeping him pinned to the carpet.

Yanking out my phone, I snarled, 'That's the least of your problems.' I let a little pressure off though. It would do me no good to be accused of excessive force.

My phone connected to the emergency line and I wasted no time attempting to explain myself. The second I got through the police dispatcher, I started talking.

'This is Tempest Michaels. I have a suspected serial killer in my custody.' I gave her the address and told her to send everything.

Only once my call was finished did I turn my attention back to the Sandman. He was trying to tell me something and had been since I threw him to the floor.

'I heard Jane say it,' he squeaked.

I narrowed my eyes. 'What?'

'The Sandman,' he attempted to clarify. 'I heard Jane say it.'

I let a little more pressure off him now, letting him fill his lungs properly.

He heaved a deep breath, and then another, before saying, 'After she tackled me to the ground and pinned me there – I must say you and your employees are very good at it – she asked Karen if she was sure I wasn't the Sandman. I guessed that was who she was employed to deal with.'

I did not like it one bit, but I was beginning to worry that I had just slammed an innocent man into his own carpet.

'You overheard Jane say the name and you just happened to guess what we are calling ... of Karen's attacker?' It was not so much that I didn't believe him, but that I didn't want to.

'Yes,' he squeaked again, craning his neck to look around and up at me. 'Is Karen all right? After the fire, she just vanished. I thought I might read about it in the paper or see her coming back to get some things, but I genuinely don't think she has returned since that night. I'm not the one you are after,' he assured me in a quiet and hopeful voice.

I closed my eyes and swore inside my head.

Retaliation

FRIDAY, DECEMBER 23RD 1735HRS

Big Ben

Jane's gran knew exactly where she had placed the note with Karen Gilbert's number on. Unfortunately, when she went to retrieve it from the small drawer in the kitchen where she kept all her odds and ends, it wasn't there.

This led to the drawer being emptied on the kitchen table and when it still didn't present itself, a thorough ransacking of the whole room ensued.

Karen Gilbert is the only person on the planet who can describe or identify the Sandman and that made her of vital importance so far as Tempest was concerned. She was in hiding and though Jane might know where she is, my impression was that no one else did and no one had a contact number for her.

We had no way to get in touch with her unless we could find the piece of paper.

Then a thought struck me: Jane's phone.

I hadn't checked her handbag to see if it was there, but I

should have. If it wasn't, and she still had it with her or near her, maybe it could be used to track her location. If it was in her handbag, maybe there would be a number for Karen Gilbert in it. Jane wrote it down for her gran, so surely she had it in her contacts log.

With that in mind, I started for the door. 'I'll be back in a minute,' I called out. 'I need to check something.'

From Basic, I got a grunt of acknowledgement, and I was out of the door.

Aylesford is built on the side of a small hill. The whole area: Maidstone, Rochester, and all the surrounding towns and villages rest atop a geographical feature known as the North Downs. They are a series of rolling hills no doubt created when one bit of land bumped into another a billion or so years ago.

Jane's gran's house was right next to the pub which is about halfway up the steepest bit of the street running through the middle of the little village. The carpark is at the bottom next to the river but there is only about a hundred and twenty yards between the two.

I set off at a jog, excited to see if I could achieve something with this field trip. Maybe if I could produce the phone number everyone wanted and get us to Karen Gilbert, I would be seen as more than just the pretty one with all the muscles.

The carpark was quiet, the sound of the river gurgling over rocks to create eddies and the sound of a couple having a row in one of the nearby houses, the only sounds to hear.

Given how quiet it was outside, it came as quite a surprise when I got ambushed.

Something inside the back of my head picked up the sound of an object travelling through the air and told me to duck. Instinct could have advised me to turn around to face the threat, but had I done that I would have got a house brick to my face.

It sailed over my head as I shot downward, smashing into my car where it shattered the driver's side window.

Well, if they wanted my attention, they had it now.

Spread out around me were a dozen men. Every last one of them wore the same black robe with the big hood and the flappy sleeves. In the middle, facing me, were Flat Top and Smiler from earlier. They were leering at me from the centre of the hemisphere surrounding my car and they had only one purpose in mind – to settle the score.

I retrieved the house brick and hefted it in one hand as I looked along the line of men.

'Feeling confident, chaps?' I asked. Before anyone could answer, I lifted the house brick to my mouth and bit off a corner. I felt the enamel on my incisors chip off and knew I would need some dentistry work to fix my perfect smile.

However, the effect on the witnesses was as intended. The smiles that dominated half a second earlier were replaced by hastily exchanged glances.

Who is this guy?

I was maybe three or four when I discovered my ability to fight. At the park with my parents, I wanted to play in the wooden fort climbing frame, but three larger boys were already in there and denied me access. I tried to push my way in and found myself shoved to the ground. It was the one and only time that has ever happened to me.

My mum saw it, and came running, my dad hot on her heels, but by the time they arrived the three boys had all run away crying. I had a broken metatarsal in my left hand from an ill-timed punch that hit the wood and not its intended target, but otherwise I was not only unscathed but imbued with a sense of what I could do. It wasn't rage that drove me to attack them with my fists, it was a sense of injustice and of moral right. What right had they to impose their will on me? If I didn't stand up to them, who would they pick on next?

It wasn't just my desire to even the scales though, I had ability to back it up. I was the tallest kid in my class by the time I started school and carried on growing. My height gave me reach, and the musculature I developed naturally was enhanced by training as my father agreed to my request to join the local kickboxing dojo.

You could say I never looked back.

That's why with odds of twelve to one, my only concern was that I might do permanent damage to someone.

You might think I would be wiser to jump into my car and get away from them, but that's just not how I am wired. Outnumbered that badly, I did the only sensible thing: I attacked.

I had no idea who these guys were – some cult of weirdos Tempest upset was my current guess - but when I sent the first two packing earlier, they went away to get reinforcements.

They should have got more.

They were spaced more or less equidistance from me and had they all moved at once, they could have attacked me simultaneously. They didn't, and before they could consider what strategy to employ, I went left, heading for the man one in from that edge of the semicircle.

It caught them all by surprise. The last thing they expected was resistance and my guess was they planned to make me apologise before giving me a fat lip anyway. None of them expected to actually have to fight and they probably all had day jobs as delivery drivers or schoolteachers or something equally benign.

The first chap had enough time to look panicked and no more. Five paces of my long legs carried me across the gap between us. I leapt into the air, throwing myself at him and powering a punch that connected with his right cheek to explode his face.

The men to his left and right had turned inward, their brains screaming for them to neutralise the menace and quickly. This was why I chose the man one in from the edge.

The one at the very end of the semicircle grabbed for me, found his arms caught in mine as I anticipated his move. Then, still using the energy in my run and punch, I pivoted off my back foot. Using it as a fulcrum, I lifted the lighter man and threw him at his colleagues. It was like playing skittles.

I figured he was close to a hundred and ninety pounds and about six feet tall. Travelling through the air three feet off the ground, he was unavoidable for the three men nearest me. That was five down in roughly three seconds and the other seven were having second thoughts.

Two of them had their feet rooted to the ground. I could ignore them because they had no interest in getting involved. That left me five.

I squared up to them, lancing out a foot to land a kick here and then another there as the fallen skittles attempted to get up. It convinced them to stay down but my focus shifted in the next instant as the second wave attacked.

Among them were the original two including the one whose nose I mashed earlier. They wanted revenge.

This time I let them come to me, reading their body language, and watching to see who would come first. You may think that one man against many can never win, but even two men trying to hit the same moving target are going to struggle and get in each other's way. When you see it on

TV or in films, it is choreographed, so, when the first came, I jinked, went under his arm, and popped up holding him.

We were chest to chest. Sure, he could kidney punch me, but he couldn't get much energy behind the blows and he was down a second later when I spun him around and into the path of a punch heading for my face.

The blow to his skull turned his lights out and the resulting crack of knuckles and squeal of pain told me another was out of the game.

I caught a blow from behind at that point, a hard fist into my left kidney and then a glancing blow on my jaw from a high elbow when I swivelled to face the attacker to my rear. The strike brought the taste of blood to my mouth but far from discouraging me, it was like injecting nitrous oxide into a car's inlet manifold.

I lunged for him, chasing as he saw the madness in my eyes and tried to get away. He couldn't back-peddle fast enough and got a hard knee between the legs for his trouble. I shoved him away to make some more space and found myself left facing just Flat Top and Smiler.

Their comrades were either down or had thought better of it and chosen to run.

As it turned out, I was wrong. The ones who were missing had gone to get weapons.

Perseverance

FRIDAY, DECEMBER 23RD 1740HRS

Jane

The rope finally broke. I heard it snap, but then I was listening for it and had been working on the last few strands for the previous five minutes.

Exhausted, sweating, and with my abs and shoulders threatening to rebel, I slid myself back out from under the bed. Panting, I gave myself a minute to recover, shuffling my bottom around until I was propped against the wall.

One loop of the rope was severed, the two pieces hanging loose and limp. I turned my hands over, inspecting the remaining loops, of which there were many, and shook my arms to see if the rope would begin to unravel.

The loose ends unwound, giving me two feet of free rope on each side, but then they stopped. The rope passed back under the other loops at that point, vanishing up between my palms and then winding around somewhere and I suspected there were other knots hidden inside because no matter what I did, I could not get the loose ends to undo any further.

My anger boiled over abruptly, the need to vent and shout and tear at the ropes too much to keep inside any longer. I thrashed, yanking my hands this way and that in a bid to get them free. They wouldn't come. All I succeeded in doing was tearing abrasions into the skin of my wrists.

When I calmed myself, sucking in fresh lungfuls of air and forcing myself to think, I could see what I needed to do. It wasn't one rope I was dealing with. It was several. It appeared to be one around each wrist, which prevented me from slipping them off. They were then linked and drawn tight by a third rope. The one I cut through was one of the ones from a wrist. I couldn't tell which one, but it hardly mattered. Now that it was loose, I needed to cut through another one. I would either get it right this time and sever the one that held my hands together, or I would get it wrong, waste half an hour, and then get it right the next time.

I knew it was a positive philosophy to go with, but as I crawled back under the bed to find the tiny burr of steel again, I knew I would rather pleasure an entire polar bear rugby team than do this again another two times.

Wasting Time

FRIDAY, DECEMBER 23RD 1741HRS

Tempest

By the time the police came, I had Harry Hengist off the carpet and sitting in a chair. He was being surprisingly generous about the event. Hilary, on my instruction, had gone back to the car. He'd taken no part in my attack and the last thing I wanted was for him to get into any bother that might impact his Christmas.

'I'm sure you meant me no harm, Tempest.' Harry insisted on using my first name though I had not invited him to do so. 'My bruises will fade.'

Was he saying it like that to make me feel bad? It was working whether he intended it to or not.

First on the scene was a squad car containing two officers I didn't recognise. They knew me though. I have an iffy relationship with the local police. Habitually, I do what I think is right and never knowingly break any laws (unless I must), but it is not unusual for me to end up in cuffs.

'Oh. It's him,' said the first cop as he exited the car.

Donning his hat, the second officer left the passenger's seat. 'This should be good.'

Having informed dispatch that I had a serial killer in custody, it came as no surprise when more flashing lights began to fill the night sky. By the time the first two officers were on Harry's garden path, two more squad cars were pulling to a halt.

Filling the doorframe as I watched them approach, I knew I was in for a dressing down or a mickey taking. One or the other, but just as I was about to step out to meet them on the path, Harry nudged my arm and came around me.

'It's all right officers,' he expressed, his tone light and jovial. 'I gave Mr Michaels cause for alarm. That's why he called you. I'm not really a serial killer though. It's kind of a funny story, actually.'

The officers didn't look like they were going to agree with him.

'You're the homeowner?' asked one. Both officers were young white men in their late twenties and filled with the righteousness of youth.

'I am,' Harry replied. 'Harry Hengist at your service.'

I was being side-lined quite deliberately. The two cops were yet to make eye contact with me, no doubt hoping I would attempt to leave so they would have reason to stop me or force my way into the conversation so they could insist I keep quiet. The pressure to move on, to continue the search for Karen Gilbert and Jane made my feet twitch, but I stayed where I was, waiting for them to get to me.

They introduced themselves to Harry as Constables Wainwright and Biggs, relaxing their postures a little but remaining all business.

Still ignoring me, Biggs turned away, using his radio to speak with dispatch and report their call out as a fake. Actually, he used the word hoax and twitched his eyes to meet mine when he said it. It felt like he was choosing to goad me, and I gave him no reaction at all.

The other cops, those who arrived in the second and third cars, were on the pavement outside the property and making no attempt to come closer. Wainwright had already informed them the call was a waste of time. They seemed content to chat about their day and take five minutes to relax before dispatch found them something else to do.

In contrast, though the call out required them to do nothing now that they were here, Wainwright and Biggs were nevertheless going through the paces. They wanted a statement from Harry and asked that we both step back inside the house. It was the first time either cop addressed me.

'What brought you to Mr Hengist's house this evening?' asked Constable Wainwright.

I had nothing to hide so I went with the blunt truth. 'There is a serial killer stalking women and murdering them.' I got a surprised but bored expression, Wainwright dismissing my claim without giving it the slightest credence. 'Chief Inspector Quinn is aware but only because I alerted him. You can refuse to believe me now, but you will hear about it from him soon enough.'

Wainwright fixed me with an even stare. 'That fails to explain your presence at Mr Hengist's house.'

'The house next door belongs to Karen Gilbert, a lady who is currently in hiding because the Sandman,' Wainwright chose to snigger at the name we had given Karen's stalker, 'had targeted her. She reported her stalker to the police,' I added, making a point and then driving it home, 'yet you chose to ignore her claims.'

Wainwright's emotionless face became a scowl. 'What

evidence do you have of any of this and what does this have to do with your presence at the property of her neighbour?' he was almost shouting.

'The investigator from my firm who handled the case went missing earlier today and I am certain the Sandman has her.' He was about to ask me another question, but I held my hand in front of his face to silence him. 'You can just believe it because I have neither the time nor the patience to explain why I know what I know. Jane Butterworth has been kidnapped and will be murdered if we fail to identify the man behind the attacks. I came here looking for clues as to the whereabouts of Karen Gilbert. Mr Hengist knew things I felt he ought not to know and that caused my call to bring you here. It would seem I was wrong, and he knew about the Sandman because he overheard Jane say the name.'

Wainwright's willingness to dismiss what I was saying was evaporating fast. I was making sense and I was known for solving cases the police were not even aware of.

'I think I need to call this in,' he said, reaching for his radio.

I took a step forward to make his hand pause. 'And I need to go. This was a dead end, but I have a team working on this problem and a dwindling clock. The Sandman is unlikely to hold her for long – at least, that is our guess. Jane is going to run out of time, and I cannot afford to waste my evening here with you.'

Surrounded

FRIDAY, DECEMBER 23RD 1742HRS

Big Ben

Emerging from the shadows at the edge of the carpark in Aylesford, four of the fake monks returned, their hands loaded with bats, crowbars and at least one machete. Those I put down in the first few seconds were getting back up, all bar the one I hit first and most firmly. He was out for the count.

All in all, even as good as I am, the odds were no longer in my favour. In fact, I'd go so far as to say I was in trouble. Even if I were also armed, the likelihood of surviving this encounter was now against me.

Grins widened as the weapons were handed out, the original two I met in the alleyway smiled the broadest.

'You should have just taken the beating,' said Flat Top. 'We only needed to take you off the playing board,' he sneered. 'Now we're going to kill you instead.'

His words confused me. He made it sound like bumping into me earlier was planned. However, there was no time for me to analyse what he meant or cross-examine him because they were coming for me.

There were ten of them now, eight or nine of whom were armed with something that could do a lot of damage. I had little choice but to turn and run.

I don't turn and run though. I never have, and I never will. I'd rather go down fighting. So I faced them, raising my hands in readiness while vainly hoping they wouldn't be brave enough to use the machete on me.

I was almost surrounded, but they did not spread out to form a complete circle. Rather, they were in clumps, sticking together because it made them feel braver to have someone at their side.

I picked a trio with bats and set my jaw as I readied myself to attack.

Basic hit all three of them in the head with a wheelbarrow.

A staccato dong, dong, dong noise filled the air as the galvanised gardening tool made short work of putting all three men down. Basic, in many ways, is the exact opposite of me. His body is made of huge lumps of blocky muscle, and his head looks like a piece of granite. In a magical world, he would be a troll and live under a bridge. I have no idea how strong he is but would not be shocked to find he could bench press more than me. The biggest difference being he could then eat the bench.

The wheelbarrow continued its swing to an accompanying 'Hur, hur,' from the man holding it by one handle. When the arc it prescribed carried him around in a circle, he launched it at another duo.

They got a nanosecond to accept they were about to be in pain before it bowled them over like twigs in a tsunami.

This was much more like it.

Basic cheered and laughed and shouted to me, 'I got der number! Granny found it on the fridge.'

Armed with that fresh piece of information, I did what I knew I ought to do and chose to call it a draw. For now. They were still armed, there were still more of them, and Jane wasn't getting saved while we were here fighting these idiots.

Gritting my teeth because I really wanted to hand out a beating now, I shouted, 'Let's go!'

Basic ran to my car, meeting me there as I yanked the driver's door open and clambered in on top of the broken glass. The window could get fixed later, right now we needed to be elsewhere.

Shouts and threats followed us as we ran away, my wheels leaving a trail of burning rubber when I stamped hard on the accelerator. I swear I almost stopped the car so I could return to finish the fight, and it was only the greater demands of the team that stopped me from doing so.

Once clear of the carpark, I checked my rear-view to see if we were being pursued. It was a genuine disappointment that we were not.

'Where do we go now?' asked Basic, still fighting to get his seatbelt on.

'Back to the office,' I told him. 'They will want that number. We just have to hope they can do something with it.'

I allowed myself a moment to get my breath back – the inevitable adrenalin caused by fighting still coursed through my body, making my pulse rate high and my breathing fast. In that quiet moment, I thought more about what Flat Top and Smiler said.

They not only made the chance encounter in the

alleyway sound planned, but he also said we were all going to pay. What did he mean by that? Who were they?

A Breakthrough, Finally

FRIDAY, DECEMBER 23RD 1746HRS

Tempest

Having dismissed their colleagues within minutes of their arrival, Constables Wainwright and Biggs now wished they hadn't. I was trying to leave, and they very much wanted me to come to the station with them. That just wasn't going to happen.

'Sir, you need to record an official statement and allow our detective branch to become involved. If, as you say, there are similar crimes going back years, and there is a serial killer in the area, they will need to know.' Both officers were blocking Harry's doorway to stop me leaving.

'Gents, your own Chief Inspector Quinn knows what I believe. I already told you that. Now I am going to leave and the only way you are going to stop me is if you choose to arrest me. I have a friend in trouble, and I am going to do what I can to help her.'

'I think you should let him go, chaps,' said Harry helpfully. 'It does sound like the police have been somewhat remiss in handling my neighbour's reports. Besides, Mr Michaels has a tough night ahead of him tonight and no doubt about it.'

My phone rang just as I was about to test the Constables' resolve and I paused to check it.

Seeing Amanda's name on the screen, I stepped back a pace and answered it.

'Amanda, have you news?'

'Tempest where are you?' Her voice came through loud and clear in the quiet hallway of Harry Hengist's house.

'I'm at Karen Gilbert's neighbour's house. I'm just about to leave,' I flicked my eyes to the cops, daring them to challenge me.

'Good. Big Ben and Basic just got back. They found all of Jane's things in her car. It was parked in Aylesford right by her gran's house, but it looks like that was where the Sandman grabbed her.' The three men in the hallway with me were all silent, each straining their ears to be able to hear Amanda's voice. 'There was no sign of a struggle according to Ben and her car was left unlocked. There's something weird though.'

I hitched an eyebrow – weird was where we started, so what did Amanda have to report that was weirder than normal?

'Go on,' I prompted.

'They were attacked.'

I snorted a laugh, imagining the pile of bodies Basic and Big Ben might have left behind.

Hearing me Amanda added, 'According to Ben they only just got away. There were a lot of them, and they were armed. He thinks it was planned.'

'Planned?' I repeated, failing to understand what she meant.

Big Ben's voice suddenly filled my ear. 'Tempest, I don't know who they were, but I think they chose to pick a fight. One said something about making us all pay – I don't think he meant just me and Basic. They also said they wanted to take me off the playing board. Any idea what that might mean?'

I was silent for a beat, my brain whirling with different ideas.

'Any idea who they were?' I wanted to know. Big Ben and I had upset various and plentiful different groups in the last few months and any of them could have chosen to take action to even the score. It could be leftover bikers from Herne Bay, or vampire wannabes. It could be the Kent League of Demonologists who we recently exposed as utter nutters. The list goes on.

Big Ben sounded disappointed when he admitted, 'None at all. I didn't recognise any of them and I didn't get a chance to ask any questions. They looked like members of a cult. If I see them again, there will be a reckoning.'

Amanda's voice echoed through my phone once more. 'Listen, we have Karen Gilbert's number. I'm going to call her as soon as I am off the phone with you. If you are done there, come back to the office. We've uncovered a few things while you've been gone.'

I sniffed in a deep breath, thankful that the other members of the team were doing better than me. The attack on Big Ben and Basic worried me but whoever his attackers were, I doubted they would be back to cause more trouble before we were finished with this case and that was all I cared about. We could deal with them later when we had more time.

As I hung up the phone, Harry clapped me on the shoulder. 'It seems your team have come through for you,

Tempest. There's something I don't understand though; why is it you want to find Karen anyway? Do you think the Sandman is still trying to target her?'

The police officers were listening to hear my answer too. 'He might be. That I cannot tell. What I believe though is that Karen Gilbert is the only person who has seen the Sandman, and I want her help to identify him. Even though she was drugged when he sang to her each time, I expect her to be able to remember his face.'

'Providing he wasn't disguised,' countered Harry.

I huffed out a hard breath of frustration. 'Provided a lot of things, actually. I won't know until I speak with her.' Switching my attention to the cops still blocking my exit, I asked, 'Are you going to try to stop me?'

They exchanged a brief glance, the two men silently asking a question of each other before Biggs spoke.

'No, we're going to return to the station,' he announced. 'Mr Hengist does not wish to press charges.'

Free to go, I shook Harry's hand and apologised once more for throwing him to the carpet.

'That's perfectly all right,' he chuckled, being more generous than I believed anyone else on the planet would be. I clapped him on the arm and left his house.

I had somewhere else to be and expected Amanda to call again any moment with an address.

Fingerprints

FRIDAY DECEMBER 23RD 1751HRS

Amanda

Big Ben's arrival back at the office caused a fresh flurry of activity. Jane's laptop and purse were laid out on Tempest's desk, the contents examined by Jagjit and Alice while I made a call.

Once I got off the phone to Tempest, I wasted no further time getting on with contacting Karen. This would be the first time I had spoken to her, and I prayed she would answer the phone even though my number would come up as unlisted. Just as I was about to press the button to connect the call, I realised I was being dumb.

From the pile of detritus found in Jane's handbag, I selected her phone and scrolled through the contacts list. There was no entry for Karen Gilbert, but I knew how protective Jane had been of Karen and how cautious her concern over the Sandman had made her.

Checking again, the piece of paper from Jane's gran in my hand, I found the same number listed under a different name. Jane had entered Karen's number under Kevin Gates. The same initials, but perhaps enough to throw someone off the scent if they grabbed her phone.

I slapped myself in the head and put the phone down.

'What is it?' asked Alice after seeing my display of self-targeted frustration.

Running from Tempest's office to my own, I called back. 'The Sandman must have touched her phone. He changed her voicemail answer message so it plays *Mr Sandman*. Chances are he had a look for Karen Gilbert's number too – I'm guessing he still plans to kill her. Either way, unless he used gloves, his fingerprints will be on it. I've stupidly been touching it, but we might get lucky.'

From my handbag, I fished a fingerprinting kit. Not one of the ultramodern ones that does it by photography and ultra-violet light, but the old-school powder and sticky tape style. It would do the trick well enough.

With the phone positioned on the desk, I put the kit down next to it and used a pen to select Kevin Gates to call – I didn't want to put off calling Karen any longer.

The phone rang and rang. In my mind, I could see Karen looking at her phone and wondering whether to answer it. Why was Jane calling her? Was it with information regarding the Sandman?

Just when I thought the phone would switch over to voicemail, it was answered, but no one spoke at the other end.

I gave it a two-count, then spoke myself, 'Karen this is Amanda Harper at Blue Moon Investigations. Jane Butterworth has been taken by the Sandman.' I blurted the words out, fearful Karen might decide it wasn't the voice she expected to hear and hang up instantly.

Another beat of silence followed before a voice at the

other end of the line finally said something. 'Jane's been taken?' Karen repeated my words as a question.

'That's what we believe. It happened earlier today. She was snatched when she got home but we don't know where she is or how long he might keep her for. We could really do with your help.'

'My help?' Karen wasn't saying much, keeping her responses short and possibly still trying to decide whether to hang up the phone or not.

I pressed on. 'I want to send Tempest Michaels to speak with you. You met him, didn't you? We are closing in on who the Sandman is,' I was exaggerating hugely, 'but if we can narrow it down, you are the only person we know of who has seen him. If we could just send you pictures ...'

Karen cut in over the top of me. 'Look, I want to help, but Jane was adamant that I should tell no one where I am and move about if possible.'

'Yes, we already tried Matilda Carpenter's house,' I let her know. 'I understand your desire to be cautious, it is absolutely the right thing to do, but we are all working on this now. We have Jane's notes and a whole team of people going through them. The police are lending officers to help us,' I added, factoring in the probability of Jan joining us soon. I wanted to call Patience, but I knew she was working and already had a bunch of reprimands against her. Sneaking off to help me might get her sacked.

'Okay,' Karen snapped out angrily. I didn't think her anger was aimed at me, but was born of frustration due to the situation she found herself in. 'Do you think you can catch him?'

'That is what we are trying to do,' I assured her without committing anything. How could I? We intended to catch him, but until we knew more than we did, our chances were slim. That is where Karen came in. 'We need your help to do it though.'

I had her on the hook and though I knew it was cruel to bring her out of hiding and to expose herself, we needed her.

'I want Tempest to call me,' she insisted. 'I'll give him my address and no one else.'

It was as good as I was going to get and I took it, thanking her for cooperating.

Disconnecting the call with another jab of the pen, I picked up my own phone and called Tempest back.

He answered before it even had a chance to ring. 'Babe.'

'I spoke with Karen, but she will only give her location to you. She knows your voice, I guess.'

He sniffed thoughtfully. 'Right. Send me her number. I'm already in the car. I'll go straight there and see if I can convince her to come back to the office with me.'

Dutifully, I sent him the contact details and crossed my fingers that she wouldn't change her mind. We needed a break in this case and soon.

Would Jane's phone provide it? I knew two chaps in the crime scene science lab who would help me out for a pack of donuts. If I could lift a fingerprint, and if the print was in the database, maybe, just maybe, we would find out who we were looking for.

I put on gloves and started with the fingerprint kit. With my eyes focused on that task, I asked Alice and Jagjit what treasures Jane's laptop had yielded.

It had been another one of Jane's clever IT ideas to install a central password override system. Each of us had our own passwords, but to protect us against exactly this type of event where the person who knew the password became unavailable, Jane created a secondary password.

Using it would unlock the computer though I don't think any of us had tested it live before today.

Jagjit and Alice were staring at the screen, the light from it illuminating their faces. 'It doesn't look like there is anything else here that we haven't already seen,' Jagjit let me know. 'The file headings are all the same, but we are going through each one to double check.'

Leaving them to continue by themselves, I started to lay out the fingerprinting kit and made a call to a pair of chaps to whom I already owed a whole bunch of favours.

Closing In

FRIDAY, DECEMBER 23RD 1812HRS

Tempest

Karen Gilbert's house is in New Ash Green which is near to nothing much at all. Though I had no idea where Karen Gilbert might be and thus which direction I would have to travel, I nevertheless chose to head back toward Rochester and the office when I left Harry Hengist's house. There was more in that direction, including the motorways.

When my phone pinged with an incoming message, I had to take my eyes off the road to squint at the screen. Hilary was holding it for me to see. It was the highly anticipated message from Amanda, which was a few words plus a number highlighted in blue and underlined – a link to make a call.

Swinging my gaze back to the road, I said, 'Punch it.'

Hilary dutifully did just that. My Porsche, apparently fixed and waiting for me to collect it – it had gotten a little busted up by some werewolves - was decked out with a hands-free kit and voice recognition. Not so the Lotus which was built before such things were dreamed of.

The number for Karen Gilbert rang once and was answered.

Timidly, a voice said, 'Hello?'

I opened my mouth to start speaking but caught myself because there was something wrong.

'That's not Karen Gilbert,' I said confidently. 'This is Tempest Michaels. Is she there?'

I heard quietly exchanged words in the background, too indistinct to make out, but a moment later a new voice came onto the phone.

'Tempest this is Karen.' My memory matched the voice I was hearing to the one I expected. 'Do you know someone called Amanda Harper?'

Nodding to myself in the dark, I admired how cautious Karen was being. 'Yes. She is my business partner. Thank you for agreeing to help.'

'Has Jane really been taken?'

This time I nodded glumly. 'Yes. I intend to get her back, but I need your help to do it.'

'Yes,' Karen sounded terrified at the prospect. 'Your colleague said you want me to help you identify him. I don't think I can do that though.'

'Why not?' I almost snapped the question at her, biting my tongue only as the words left my mouth.

She sighed with frustration of her own. 'Because I never really got a good look at him. I explained this to Jane at the time. I was always immobile in bed, unable to move yet conscious enough to hear him. Looking down my nose at him while I was in bed and he was sitting in the chair across my bedroom, I got an impression of his face, but I wouldn't be able to pick him out of a line up.'

I had to unclench my hands from the steering wheel I was gripping it so tightly. I could not recall a case that defied me more than this one. There had to be a chink in his armour, a way to work out who he was and how he selected his victims.

'I need to meet you tonight,' I stated boldly. 'You want this to end as much as I do. Together we can work out who he is and get him locked up once and for all.'

She said nothing for several seconds, making me wait while she tried to decide whether to trust me or not. Possibly feeling like she had no way out of this nightmare unless she faced it, she reluctantly agreed.

'I'm staying at number fifteen Iden Rise in Harrietsham. What car are you driving? I will look out for it.'

Harrietsham wasn't hard to find, but it wasn't close either. From where we were, I figured it would take most of an hour to get to.

I said as much, adding a promise to get there as swiftly as I could. Once the call disconnected, Hilary set the satnav on his phone to find the address she gave us.

It confirmed my guess, estimating the time to destination at fifty-six minutes. It was already mid evening, and I was no closer to achieving anything. Was Jane even still alive?

A New Challenge

FRIDAY, DECEMBER 23RD 1836HRS

Jane

If I thought my arms, shoulders, and abs hurt before, it was nothing compared to the screamingly intense misery I felt now. I would sooner have tried to circumcise myself with a soldering iron than commit to cutting through a third rope.

The second rope gave with a twang as it parted, the two ends finally giving up their fight and I felt an instant change in the ropes holding my hands together.

I almost whooped with joy and probably would have done if I didn't already feel like crying. What I did do was sag, letting my whole body go floppy as I relaxed every muscle. Lying under the bed, willing myself to get moving again, I tried hard to not think about how much I still needed to do. Getting my hands free was reason to celebrate, but if I couldn't get out of my cell, it did little to improve my situation.

What surprised me was the Sandman not coming to see

what I was doing. He had been able to see and hear me until I covered over the lens of the camera, effectively blinding him. Even so, I had been making grunting noises for more than an hour as I fought to cut through the ropes around my wrists and surely the lack of camera feed would make him want to check on me.

The questions about where I was and whether he was able to watch me the whole time remained.

After a minute of getting my breath back, I shimmied out from under the bed and prayed I never had to go under there again.

The ropes around my wrists were loose but they didn't cooperate and fall straight off. It took a further ten minutes of biting them and pulling with my teeth to feed the loose pieces back through the remaining knots. Each time I got another loop off, my wrists came farther apart until they were suddenly free.

In a flurry of movement, I shed the ropes, multiple lengths of it falling to land at my feet as I pushed myself upright. I was battered and bruised, but I was free of my restraints and ready to inflict pain if I got the chance.

My friends would be coming for me, that much I was certain of. Tempest and Amanda, Big Ben probably, and whoever else they could drum up to help. If Jan knew, he would lend his help too. Maybe they would find me before I needed to escape. Maybe when the door opened it wouldn't be the Sandman standing outside, but my handsome boyfriend here to rescue me.

These were positive thoughts, and they buoyed me up as I turned my attention to the door.

I like to think that I am fairly good with computers. It's mostly self-taught but I found their inner workings and how the operating systems function simple to grasp and then manipulate. I enjoyed it too, but the electronics for a door, vastly simpler in design no doubt, well I had no idea how that worked.

Steely Eyed Thief Taker

FRIDAY, DECEMBER 23RD 1842HRS

Quinn

Chief Inspector Quinn had spent the last two hours going over the information Tempest Michaels sent him and the last ten minutes swearing. So far as Ian Quinn was concerned the reasons to dislike the local paranormal detective were long and varied. However, his annoying habit of being right was at the top of the list.

River Tam, a woman found in a field two years ago was an unsolved case. Had it been his case, the blemish would not have been tolerated, but since it impacted a different senior officer in a different district of Kent, he hadn't given it a moment's thought and could only vaguely recall the case now.

She had been murdered, injected with a drug that shut down her respiratory system. The file from Tempest suggested there were two dozen other cases. On the face of it, they were all recorded as missing persons, the ladies vanishing as so many did each year. However, when examined with a less cynical eye, Quinn could draw similarities that linked their disappearances.

He even recalled some of the names and it went back more than twenty years. The women were all similar in appearance and age. All lived alone and all just up and vanished one day. Checking the filed missing person reports was a simple matter. Family members came forward to state their daughter/sister/whatever had gone missing but in the police reports that followed, there was never any suggestion of foul play.

Their homes had not been broken into; there was no sign of a struggle. Their cars were generally found still in their garage or parked outside their house. There was nothing to suggest to the police that a crime had been committed and therefore no investigation followed.

However, now that he was looking deeper, half a dozen of the women reported having a stalker at some point in the weeks or months leading up to their disappearance. In the last two hours, Quinn found three separate reports from the last decade in which the women reported someone being in their house at night and singing to them. It was always the same song. That the reports were not linked to the missing person reports prevented anyone from following up, and they came from all over Kent which meant different officers in different departments had filed the reports. Twenty years ago, there was no central database, but even now, such a tenuous link was unlikely to be spotted.

How he hated that Tempest Michaels was right.

What to do about it though? How could he turn this into a personal win? There was a simple and immediate answer to that question – he needed to let Tempest Michaels lead him to the so-called Sandman and swoop in to make the arrest with his men.

With the evidence Tempest Michaels so generously sent him, he could claim it was his department's fine detective work, undertaken in secrecy to protect ... he couldn't remember the name of the woman from New Ash Green but remembered that was when he first heard the name Sandman. He clicked back into the file, searching until he found the name he wanted. It would be a simple thing to claim to his superiors his investigation had to remain secret even from them. He had been ensuring Karen Gilbert remained safe from the serial killer.

A smile tugged at the corners of his mouth. Catching a serial killer, that was going to ensure his next promotion. It was the sort of bust that became legendary. Fellow officers would refer to him as a *steely-eyed thief taker* or *the man who put the Sandman to sleep*.

'Ooh, that's catchy,' he said to himself.

Pushing away from his desk, he went in search of Sergeants Faraday and Kenya. They were two of his finest, by which he meant they could be relied upon to do exactly as he said and follow him to the top by riding his shirt tails.

Ambition. Some saw it as a bad thing, but Chief Inspector Ian Quinn knew it was what made him great. He was a great cop because he had ambition. Using Tempest Michaels to aid his climb up the ranks was no different to a great craftsman selecting the right tool from his box.

According to the annoying Mr Michaels, his odd cross-dressing assistant, James Butterworth, was to be the Sandman's next victim. That had to be avoided at all costs, not because Quinn cared what happened to him; he could not have cared less. He needed to prevent it if possible because Butterworth reporting it was the police who saved him would put Tempest's nose out of joint and sound better than Quinn reporting his own glory.

Then again, a voice in Quinn's head argued, a fresh grisly murder always grabs the front page. If you catch the killer right afterwards ...

Happy with either scenario, he clicked his fingers to get the attention of one of his officers.

Start Talking, Punk!

FRIDAY, DECEMBER 23RD 1903HRS

Tempest

About halfway to Harrietsham, it was silent in the car. Hilary wasn't much of a conversationist and I was lost in my own thoughts. Currently, I was thinking about Big Ben's random and unexpected attack earlier. If there was a gang targeting us, the chance of them finding me could not be ignored. A worrying voice reminded me my home was undefended and that caused me to call Mrs Comerforth.

The lady in the house next to mine considered herself too old to own a dog but loved looking after my miniature Dachshunds. In the recent weeks, they had been in her house so often it was beginning to feel like joint ownership.

My pair of black and tan sausages were easy company for her and thus leaving them snoozing on her couch was a mutually beneficial arrangement. However, she tended to put them back in my house at bedtime in anticipation that I would come home and want to find them there.

Not only was I doubtful I was going home tonight, I was also now worried someone might target it.

I had Hilary call her with my phone, my right foot getting heavier on the accelerator now that I didn't have a squad car tailing me.

She answered with, 'Good evening, Tempest, are you home already, dear?'

I could picture her watching her evening soaps with my dogs snoring either side of her lap. Dozer was most likely upside down with his top lip hanging loose to reveal his scary fangs – he's about as scary as an enraged cheese sandwich. Bull would be more alert, poised in case there was food or to repel an intruder if someone were to knock on the door.

'Good evening,' I replied. 'I'm afraid I might not make it home at all tonight. Would it be inconvenient for you to keep the boys at your house until the morning?'

'Not at all, dear. They just sleep on the couch when I go up to bed. Are you chasing a maniac?'

'I'm sorry?'

'A maniac,' Mrs Comerforth repeated. 'It seems you are always trying to catch some maniac who is doing something evil and twisted.'

I could not recall ever discussing my work with my neighbour, but then my line of work is hardly a secret. I had to assume I was talked about in whatever circles she moved or maybe she just reads the paper.

To give her an answer, I said, 'Yes, I guess you could say that.'

'Well, take care then, dear. Try not to get hurt. I'll bring them around in the morning if your car is on the driveway.'

That was the dogs taken care of then. With the call ended, I asked, 'How much longer to our destination?'

Hilary picked up his own phone and poked it to bring it back to life.

'Fourteen minutes.'

'Can you call Amanda for me, please?'

Hilary switched phones again, set it to speaker and held the phone in the middle of the car. 'Hey, babe,' Amanda's all too sexy voice filled my car's interior. It wasn't her intention to use a bedroom voice, only that my brain heard it that way. All the time. It is so distracting.

I glanced at Hilary to find his cheeks burning. Maybe it wasn't just in my head then.

'Are you at Karen's yet?' she asked.

'Nearly. A few more minutes. I'll confirm when I have her.'

'Are you planning to bring her back to the office?' Amanda sounded surprised by the concept.

'Yes. I need her to look at pictures. Plus, if she is with us, I will know not to worry about her. She's been in hiding for weeks which makes this the first time she has raised her head above the parapet since she fled her house. That has to make her nervous.'

'I guess.' Amanda sounded less sure. 'What do we do with her if we all leave the office. If we get an address for the Sandman, she is not going to want to come with us.'

That was a fair point.

'We give her to Big Ben?' I suggested.

It got a laugh from my girlfriend at least. Big Ben would charm Karen's knickers off in under a minute. However, if we were to raid the Sandman's lair, he would be coming with us. Heck, I doubted I could leave him behind if I tried. Plus, he is like employing a siege weapon. I wouldn't want to break into anywhere without him because that would be like owning a bazooka and opting to not take it to a battle.

Coming up with a better plan, I said, 'We can have Patience pick her up, or leave her with Jagjit and Alice. It's not an issue I need to deal with yet, so I guess I am happy to ignore it until I do.'

Amanda had no argument to offer and more pressing things to tell me. 'We've been looking at neighbours for the ladies in Jane's file. We went through relatives and jobs, co-workers, et cetera. So far finding any kind of pattern or link is defying us. They all come from different areas, they all had different jobs ... there's nothing we can find that would tie them together or single them out.'

'But unless his targets are completely random, he found a reason to target each of these women,' I concluded the point she was making.

'That's right. Whoever he is, he came into their lives and chose to kill them. That they all look alike cannot be coincidence either and there has to be something in that.'

'Except you cannot find anything that links them so far.'

'No,' she agreed, sounding frustrated. 'Not so far. That's why we are looking at neighbours. It goes back to what you said about someone having a key. It feels like a long shot though. Big Ben has a theory about the Sandman being a locksmith.'

'Not exactly a theory,' I heard Big Ben's voice in the background. 'More of a wild stab in the dark.'

I ran the idea through my head. 'I guess that makes sense. A locksmith would be able to pick a lock or know how to get around one.'

Amanda said, 'It's on our board. It's another reason we are looking at neighbours, but I worry that Big Ben could be right. If it's a locksmith doing this, then he might have met the women on a callout to fix a lock and there will be no traceable record of that happening.'

I pursed my lips and wished I had something to kick.

Changing the subject, I asked, 'Anything from Jan yet?'

Jane's boyfriend would drop whatever he was doing and race to help us I had no doubt. Only if we got hold of him though.

Amanda's voice came back with a side order of severely irked. 'No, and it's starting to bother me. I called the station again; he's not on shift tonight. I'm thinking of going to his apartment to hammer on the door.'

'I'll go,' offered Big Ben, his voice easy to make out as it came through Amanda's phone. 'There's a key to his apartment on Jane's bunch. I noticed it when I took them from her car.'

'Did you hear that?' Amanda asked.

A cop in our corner wouldn't hurt at all. 'Do it.' It might be a wasted trip, or it might bolster our numbers and provide a new element with contacts inside the local police. Either way, it felt better to be doing something.

Amanda's voice came back on the phone. 'He just left with Basic. Jan's probably just asleep with his phone off. I remember how tired I used to be after a run of shifts.'

The call had eaten up most of the remaining journey time and I was leaving the motorway. Wanting to be able to concentrate on the directions, I wished everyone back at the office better luck and got off the phone.

Harrietsham was not a place I knew, nor one I believed I had ever been to before. That it was unfamiliar mattered not in the era of satellite navigation as Hilary's phone's built-in system took us directly to the address Karen gave.

The street was lit much like the last one in New Ash Green, Christmas lights making the houses look inviting and warm. It wasn't hard to imagine the palpable excitement bubbling away inside those houses with children inside. As I pulled to a stop, I got the notion that I might enjoy being a father. The idea snuck up and jumped out on me, catching me by surprise and I thought that it was perhaps the first-time parenthood had ever occurred to me as an attractive possibility.

There being no time to dwell on such things, I checked my watch, patted my pockets to make sure I had all my things and swung the door open. Hilary bailed from his side, fighting to get his feet under his backside as the car delivered him almost level with the pavement.

The house to my front had a driveway with a single car parked on it. There were lights on in the back that shone through vaguely to the frosted glass in the front door but for the most part, it did not look like there was anyone home.

I was expecting there to be someone watching for my arrival but looking for a tell-tale twitch of a curtain in any of the windows facing out to the street, I saw nothing.

'It's awfully quiet,' observed Hilary.

Alert as I walked up the driveway toward the front door – which is to say I was looking for danger – I felt the person approaching before I saw them. Someone was moving stealthily, sneaking up on us from behind a clipped hedge at the property's boundary.

I lifted my left hand to my face, a single finger in front of my lips as I silently begged Hilary stay quiet. His eyes went wide, and I saw him gulp with nervousness.

My shoulder bag came over my head to be set down on the ground as I slid soundlessly into the shadow thrown by the hedge.

When the person – a man, I could tell the moment his lead foot came into view – slunk around the edge of the twiggy shrub, I struck.

Good timing and the element of surprise gave me all

the advantage I needed. The man, overweight by fifty pounds or more reeled backward and squealed in fright when I suddenly appeared in front of his face but by then it was too late.

I already had hold of his coat and was converting his backward motion into a throw. Yanking him off balance, I planted my feet and spun. He went over my legs, falling and twisting at the same time to land on the driveway with a hard thump.

The air rushed from his lungs in a whoosh, and I heard his head crack on the solid concrete surface. It was the perfect time to follow up with blows to soft body parts such as his throat, eyes, and groin, but I had no idea who he was and had already tackled one innocent person today.

I stepped to his side to make striking with his feet less easy and loomed over him, looking down with threatening malice on my lips.

'Start talking,' I insisted.

Hilary came at him from the other side, a snarl on his lips. 'Yeah, punk! Start talking.'

I had to hitch an eyebrow at my partner but didn't get to say anything to his odd display of machismo because a voice called out from the across the street.

It was accompanied by a squeal of horror. 'Tempest! Don't hurt him!'

I stepped back and away from the fallen man, taking myself out of strike range while also keeping him in sight. Doing so allowed me to swing my attention to the two women running across the road.

One was Karen Gilbert.

Putting two and two together fast, I said, 'You're not staying in this house at all are you?'

The woman with her had to be the man's girlfriend or

wife; she ran straight to his side to check his condition. Karen came to me.

'Sorry,' she apologised. 'It felt safer to lie about the address and then be able to watch who turned up. Just in case, you know?'

I nodded and turned my attention to the man on the ground and offered him my hand to get up. 'Are you okay, big fella? I hope I didn't damage anything.'

He was doing his best in front of the ladies to pretend it didn't hurt – I would have done the same. Thankfully, he took my hand and didn't appear to hold a grudge.

'That was quite the move you put on me,' he said.

'I caught you by surprise, that's all. You probably would have snuck up on me, but I was already watching for someone to attack when I arrived.' Okay, so I was being generous – this wasn't a competition, and I thought it likely the man had gamely volunteered to be the one to make first contact with me.

Karen did some quick introductions. 'Tempest this is Marion and Buck. I went to university with them both. They have generously been letting me live here for the last week.'

I shook Buck's hand and gestured with my eyes into the darkened street. 'Which one of these is yours then?'

Their home was across the street in a diagonal line. From it, they had been able to see us arrive and send Buck to intercept. He was supposed to bring us back to their place. No one expected me to tackle him.

Safely inside their house, Karen wanted a full breakdown of what had been going on, what happened to Jane and why I thought I was going to be able to do what the police were not even trying to achieve.

'I think that last bit might change,' I let her know. 'I

think the police are going to get on board quite fast now.' Seeing that she wanted more explanation than that, I said, 'I threw the gauntlet down at one of the local senior officers. He and I do not get on very well and he wants nothing more than to stop me from successfully exposing a killer that he knows he ought to be pursuing. If I know the man at all, he'll be forming a secret taskforce to identify the Sandman right now.'

'That doesn't help Jane though,' she pointed out.

We were in Marion and Buck's kitchen, leaning against the counters while Marion made coffee.

I decided not to hide the truth from Karen. 'I am worried for Jane. She is resourceful but if we cannot find him and therefore her, she will have to fight him alone and he may have kept her unconscious.'

Karen's eyes widened. 'You think she's already dead?'

I gave her a grim expression by way of reply. 'I doubt he plans to keep her alive. If she is still alive, then she is in serious trouble. I need you to come back to the Blue Moon office. We are working on this problem to the detriment of all other cases, and I want you to help us identify who he is.'

Karen's face was white with fear and horror at the thought of the Sandman killing Jane, but it flushed with colour now as she recoiled from my request.

'What? No! No way! I'm not leaving this house!'

I had to raise my hands in a bid to calm her, but I was too late, and she was already starting to hyperventilate.

Dancing to my Tune

FRIDAY, DECEMBER 23RD 1922HRS

The Sandman

'What do you mean you weren't able to take them? You said there were only two of them.' He was anxious to return to check on his captive but there was something far more important he needed to do first.

Finally, he was going to be able to save Karen. That she had been hiding from him was typical of all the girls he saved. None of them understood the gift he was giving them until it had been given, but that was what made him so special. It was how he had drawn a small army of followers to aide him in his quest.

They were foot soldiers, nothing more, but useful for what they could do. They all had dirty pasts, filled with crime and lustful thoughts. None of them were pure like him, but then the pure would be too good to waste and he liked how disposable his foot soldiers were.

What he did not like, was the incompetence.

'There were only two of them, master, but they are not

normal men. They fought back with the strength of a hundred and one used a wheelbarrow.'

'A wheelbarrow?' Had his ears deceived him?

'Yes, master. They are not to be underestimated.' The man making the excuses was Paul Sutcliffe. The same man who Big Ben chose to name Smiler. He was one of the master's longest serving followers and proud to be considered loyal. The master had promised him a kill soon and he intended to remain worthy.

The Sandman did not underestimate the Blue Moon team. Not one bit. That they had been able to come as close as they had when the police had never so much as detected his existence spoke volumes. He'd met two of them and was impressed by both. Not so impressed that he cared to change his plans though. The woman, Jane Butterworth, was already his captive and soon the others would fall into the neat trap he'd set in motion.

The man waiting for instruction was just another acolyte, an employee he'd handpicked for his very specific set of skills. They were all alike, his followers, all looking for something to give their lives purpose and all without a rudder to help them steer through life.

He became that rudder for them. They were criminals, lowlifes with no skills or qualifications to give them hope for a better future. He gave them that too, seducing them with all that he promised before exposing them to the truth of what they needed to do to obtain it.

They did not all accept his gift, but those who did not were few and soon dealt with by those who already had. The secret of their society protected them all.

Now the Blue Moons threatened it.

Allowing his thoughts to return to the man on the

phone, the Sandman commanded, 'Go to the woods. Make preparations.'

Paul frowned in his lack of understanding. 'They will come to us?'

'I have foreseen it.' He hadn't foreseen anything, but his planning allowed for someone to figure out who he was. Despite his care over the years, there was always the danger his mission would be misunderstood, and his work condemned. Expecting it allowed him to plan. Part of that plan made the foot soldiers necessary. Another part was the trap he was leading Tempest Michaels and his friends into. They would all die and what they might have discovered would vanish with them.

In awe of his master's powers and wisdom, the acolyte said, 'As you command, so I will obey.'

With the conversation complete, the Sandman put down the phone and drew in a slow breath. He knew Jane Butterworth was up to something in her cell, but he wasn't there to determine what it might be. She was doing things that most others hadn't and had blinded him to her activities somehow.

There was a need to return to her location. He doubted she could do what no other ever had, but why risk it. He would go soon.

He checked his camera feed again. It was the same blackness it had been since just after he left her in the building more than an hour ago. Since leaving, every time he checked on her, he could hear grunting and straining. Oddly, she sounded more like a man than a woman as she fought to get free of her bindings, for that was what he felt certain she was doing.

Confused, he checked the feed to his second victim, the one he took as a precaution, but that one was still unconscious, the camera feed showing the still form lying on the bed. He shrugged, accepting that he overestimated the dose of etorphine to administer. It wasn't a problem; there was plenty of time before the ceremony for the drug to work itself out of his body.

Jane was fighting to get free. The thought brought a smile to his face. How far would she be able to get? Taking her was the right thing to do, of course, no one could argue that.

He expected the Blue Moon team would pick up on their colleague's absence and that in turn would make them look hard at his case. Ultimately, there was a purpose to their inclusion, and it was an important one. It exposed a danger they might uncover his identity, and that was why he planned to kill them all. However, they would give him that which he could not get for himself.

His foot soldiers were deployed to slow them down, the less important pieces anyway. That giant brute was supposed to end up in hospital and for his injuries to look like a random altercation. There were teams deployed to several obvious locations, Jane Butterworth's house being just one of them. Had it been Tempest who arrived there, they would have left him alone. However, it hadn't been and his instructions on the matter were simple. That they failed to remove the big one from the board was unacceptable.

However, the same acolyte leading the charge there, had earlier succeeded in placing the tracking device on Tempest Michaels. The Sandman switched to a different app, checking the Blue Moon's lead investigator's location.

A smile crept across his face because he was right about the biggest reason to take Jane Butterworth. She was an outlier – someone he would not normally have taken an interest in. Only when she denied him Karen Gilbert did he choose to save her.

It wasn't really about saving Jane though; he took her to set in motion a series of events that would lead him back to Karen Gilbert.

Looking down at the map in his hand and the dot blinking away at its centre, he knew he had to postpone returning to check on his current captives. There could be only one reason why Tempest had gone out tonight – he was visiting Karen Gilbert.

Her disappearance had been most bothersome, yet in many ways, being made to wait made saving her more satisfying. His acolytes had already tracked Tempest to one address only to discover Karen wasn't there. They were trailing him still, so perhaps Harrietsham, where the paranormal P.I. was currently shown to be, would reveal Karen's secret location.

He would know soon enough.

More Bad News

FRIDAY, DECEMBER 23RD 1933HRS

Big Ben

Jan Van Doorn's apartment is in a block of flats near Tovil. More accurately, it was near the dodgy end of Tovil just outside the city centre. One only had to travel about another mile to find wide open countryside and beautiful detached houses with swimming pools and expensive cars parked on the drive. On a drive in Tovil, one was more likely to find an old refrigerator with a couple of drunk fourteen-year-old kids sitting on it.

My car with its broken window was going to fit right in.

Sticking my head out of the hole where the glass should be, I scanned the ugly, square block of flats for a name to confirm I had the right building and stopped the car.

'Dis it?' asked Basic, happily playing a *Gameboy* in the passenger seat.

I squinted into the dark, looking for movement or signs that there might be anyone here waiting for us.

When I was content we were not going to find a fresh ambush awaiting us, I said, 'Yes,' and got out of the car.

Basic followed suit, pocketing his electronic toy and pushing his sleeves up to his elbows. I guess he had the sense that there might be more trouble too.

The building sat dark and quiet. On the Friday before Christmas there ought to be more noise and more people. There were lights in a lot of the windows, not just of the flats but also of the houses around us. There were very few decorations outside though, most likely because they would be stolen in seconds. Or already had been.

The main door was fitted with an electronic lock to keep unwanted people out. Surprisingly, it worked. They are easy enough to defeat, especially if you have someone like Basic around, but there was an easier way to get in than breaking the lock.

I jabbed a bunch of the buzzers, alerting the residents in about twenty different random apartments.

Several answered at once, to which I replied, 'Pizza,' and heard the pop and buzz as the door was opened.

Thereafter, it was a simple case of climbing the stairs to find Jan's apartment. His door was locked, and no one came to answer it when we thumped as hard as we dared. I didn't want to draw unnecessary attention to our presence so shouting through the door to wake Jan up – if he were in there asleep – was not a good option.

Instead, I used the key I found on Jane's bunch of keys. It was helpfully labelled, *Jan's place*.

A neighbour's door opened across the landing and a woman popped her head out. We had made enough noise to make her curious. Seeing me put a key in Jan's lock, her face took on a worried expression. I think it was largely caused by Basic's rolled up sleeves. He looked like a crap hitman escaped from a nineties film. He also looked like a bear and a caveman had a child and someone had then put clothes on it, so I wasn't surprised by her reaction.

With a turn of the key, the door opened, and I swung it wide with a gesture that Basic should go inside. Then I hit the lady with a smile and started walking her way. She was maybe twenty-five or twenty-six, had freckles that went with her strawberry blonde hair, and she was dressed for a night out.

It was mid-evening, so she probably had a friend or friends over for a few drinks to get them going before they grabbed a taxi into the city centre to hit a nightclub or two.

This was going to be easy.

Widening my smile, I said, 'Hey, babe. I'm Big Ben, but I guess you already worked that part out for yourself.' She lifted an eyebrow. 'Did you have plans over Christmas that included screaming my name multiple times? Because you do now.'

A second lady appeared next to the first, confirming my theory about having friends over for drinks first. She was mixed race, African and Chinese perhaps. Whatever her racial origins, she was a knockout. I hit her with the same smile.

'That goes for you too, kitten.'

She curled her lip at me, 'Oh, wow, what a creep you are.'

This happens occasionally, and I mean occasionally. So rare that I forget it even can happen, but I was being knocked back.

Caught off guard, I mumbled, 'Excuse me?'

The mixed-race lady hooked her friend's arm, guiding

her back inside the flat with a sneer thrown in my direction. As the door slammed shut on my face, I heard her say, 'Old men are such pigs.'

'Old men?' I repeated, still staring at the closed door. Okay, I'm not in my twenties anymore. I'm not even in my early thirties but why would that matter when I look this good?

They were clearly lesbians. At least that's what I told myself as I wandered thoughtfully back to Jan's front door. It was that or I was losing my touch. First the girls outside gran's house in Aylesford and now this. It was unprecedented, but it wasn't the start of a trend and nothing you can say would convince me otherwise.

Still, the word *old* was going to stick in my head for a while.

I found Basic standing in the middle of Jan's living space.

'Did you do this?' I asked.

Basic looked at me, his eyebrows doing a little dance as he tried to figure out what I was asking.

'The destruction?' I waved my right arm to indicate the desolation of Jan's apartment.

'Wasn't me,' Basic rumbled.

I walked through to the bedroom and checked in the bathroom and tiny broom closet by the door. I wanted to be certain Jan's body wasn't stuffed somewhere before I spoke to anyone. His apartment had been turned upside down but not like it had been burgled. It looked like there had been a struggle. It didn't extend beyond the central living space, but that area was trashed.

A wireless speaker had been knocked off a shelf and was broken on the floor. Two potted plants had followed it.

The TV was askew, and framed photographs had been knocked from one wall. No attempt had been made to tidy up, the perpetrators choosing to leave as quickly as possible.

With a frustrated sigh that rippled my lips, I took out my phone to make a call.

Toby Carter

FRIDAY, DECEMBER 23RD 1940HRS

Amanda

'Here's something.'

Jagjit's announcement brought my head up from the screen and the boring-as-wallpaper report I was reading. The search for information had got us nothing but sore eyes and stiff necks so far. I was on my fifth or sixth cup of coffee and I knew none of us were going to stop until we found Jane.

That Jane might already be dead was something none of us were prepared to voice. Tempest was with Karen Gilbert; he'd sent a text to confirm he'd found her, and we were pulling together pictures of men who we believed met the right demographic.

Unfortunately, all we had to base that demographic on was a description Karen Gilbert gave Jane three weeks ago.

'What is it, Jagipoos?' asked Alice, the man's wife employing what had to be one of the world's worst pet names ever.

He was working in Tempest's office, trawling through ... something. I'd lost track of what each of us was working on. I left my office to join him.

'I've been looking at neighbours,' he announced.

'We all have,' Alice reminded him.

He looked at her and blinked twice. 'Their properties specifically, I mean. Would you believe there is a chap who was a neighbour to River Tam who was also living right next door to Naomi Parker fifteen years ago when she went missing?'

This was big news! I'd been lounging in the door waiting to hear what he might have to say. Now I was bumping hips with him because I needed to see what he had found.

Alice hit him from the other side, the pair of us ladies making a sandwich filling of Tempest's Indian friend.

See this guy,' he pointed to a name: Toby Carter. 'I mean, it could be coincidence - I don't have a photograph for comparison, but the names are the same. Is this the sort of thing you were looking for?'

The question was aimed at me and though it was too early to get excited, I could already feel my pulse beginning to race.

'This is exactly the sort of thing I was hoping to find.' I was staring at the name, feeling it etch itself indelibly into my brain. 'We need to focus on him now, find out if he pops up again anywhere else. Can I leave you doing that, Jagjit?'

'Sure, I'll stay on it,' he promised me, sounding equally excited though he was probably picking up on the emotion coming from me.

Alice asked, 'What do you need me to do?'

I started toward the door. 'You and I are going to trawl

the internet for Toby Carters, and we are going to find this guy.'

Hurrying after me, Alice questioned, 'Won't there be hundreds of them? That doesn't sound like a rare name.'

I agreed. 'Probably, but we know his rough age and we know he is local. Unless we are unlucky, we will eliminate all but one or two in just a few minutes. You tackle social media, I'll go on *LinkedIn*. He has to show up somewhere.'

Alice jogged back to the reception desk to work on the computer there and I placed a call to Simon and Steven in the crime lab.

Simon answered. 'Ah, Amanda. I was just about to call you.'

'You have identified the fingerprint?' I was literally holding my breath.

Simon cleared his throat. 'I have, yes.'

I waited a beat, expecting him to say a name or tell me he was just emailing over a file. When I got nothing, I blurted, 'Well, who is it, Simon?'

I could hear Steven chuckling in the background when Simon said, 'My colleague advises me to hold the name to ransom until doughnut payment is made.'

I closed my eyes and tried to stay calm. 'Simon, I cannot express how urgently I need that information. I'll pay you double. I'll pay you triple. Heck, I'll buy out the doughnut store if I need to, but I have to have that name and I need it now!' By the time I finished ranting, my calm had dissolved, and my voice was close to a shout.

Simon said, 'Whoa! Okay, Amanda.'

I needed them far more than they needed me, and I was leveraging their good nature to get them to do things that might get them in trouble.

'I'm sorry, Simon. I just really need that name and

whatever else you have on the person. One of my friends has been kidnapped and I think the fingerprint comes from the person responsible.'

Desperately hoping he would say, 'Toby Carter,' it felt like a punch to the gut when he said, 'Ramsey Mitchell. Aged sixty-three. He was booked for shoplifting in 1974. Nothing since. I'll send you over the file. Usual email address, yes?'

'Yes, please,' I sagged, wishing I hadn't shouted at him. 'I'm sorry I shouted.'

'Don't worry about it. I should have known you would need it urgently. You wouldn't trouble us otherwise. I'm sending it over now,' he assured me.

'I'll bring the doughnuts by as soon as I can.'

'That's okay,' he laughed. 'My wife says I am getting fat. I don't dare tell her I have a young, blonde woman buying me sweet treats. You can have this one for free. There's already enough sugar in my house to sink a ship. Have a good Christmas.'

I heard Steven in the background echoing his work partner's sentiments, thanked them profusely, and got off the phone. Rushing to my desk, I found the email waiting for me.

Before I could read it, Jagjit called out, 'I found another one.'

Defeated

FRIDAY, DECEMBER 23RD 1942HRS

Tempest

The call from Big Ben interrupted me before I could get to the point where I started begging Karen to see sense. She was terrified to do anything other than hide in her friends' house. That didn't work for me, but I didn't feel that physically dragging her with me was a move I could allow myself to make.

She was looking at me with accusing eyes as if I were the one threatening her life, and Marion had called Buck to come back to the kitchen. I was terrorising their guest and they were going to ask me to leave.

Hilary was keeping quiet, wishing he'd stayed at the office probably.

Trying to figure out something I could say that might make her change her mind, or to come up with a way to make this work without her leaving the house, I lifted my phone to my ear.

Buck was getting hastily whispered instructions from

The Sandman

Marion, but I turned away and put Hilary between us so he couldn't so easily speak to me.

To Big Ben I said, 'What have you got?'

Bluntly he replied, 'Jan Van Doorn has been kidnapped.' He fell silent, expecting me to say something no doubt but my mind was swirling like a hurricane just blew through it. 'Are you there?' he questioned.

'Yup,' I muttered. 'How sure are you?'

'It's a guess,' he admitted. 'His place is trashed though, and it looks like a fight, not a burglary. My guess is the Sandman got here first. Jan's phone is on the couch, so I think it's unlikely he went out and this happened afterward.'

Hilary was frowning at me, wanting to know what was causing my brow to furrow so.

'The Sandman,' I repeated for Hilary to hear. I was staring into nothing and beginning to sound like I'd been lobotomised. 'Why?' A better question might have been how but they both amounted to the same thing. If this was the Sandman, and I understood his particular serial killer pattern correctly, there had never been a man taken before.

But what if I was wrong? What if Jane hadn't found any men because she hadn't been looking for them. I saw two dozen women in Jane's file. What if there was an equal number of men? If I accepted that Jan had been taken by the Sandman, I also had to assume it was because the Sandman had taken Jane.

The exact detail of what he planned to do with them was the stuff of nightmares and insignificant to the problem at hand which remained our need to identify, track and catch the maniac.

'I need to report this to the police,' I mumbled.

Big Ben came to my rescue. 'I'll do it. I'm going to do it from the office though, or at least not from inside his apartment. I don't want to get caught up answering questions and making statements tonight.'

I gave that just a few seconds thought, then argued. 'No, I'll do it. I'm going to speak to Quinn. The police need to get on board, and this might tip the balance.'

Karen overheard me. 'You said the police were already involved. Were you lying to me?'

Cursing myself, I ended the call quickly. 'Ben, I have to go. Call Amanda, see how she is getting on and head back to the office if that is where she needs you. I'll be there as soon as I can.'

'How's it going with Karen?' he asked, but I cut him off before he could finish asking the question.

Karen's eyes had been accusing before. Now they were livid. I was going to try to calm her down, but I didn't hold out much hope.

'What I said was the senior police officer has the file and would be throwing officers at the case.'

'But you don't know that he is doing anything, do you?' Karen raged.

Hilary tried to calm things down. 'We are only trying to help.'

He got completely ignored by everyone.

Buck took a step forward, though not in a threatening manner – I'd already put him on his backside once this evening. Rather, he was attempting to get his bulk between me and the ladies in the house.

'I think perhaps you had better go now,' he suggested, his tone making it sound like a hopeful plea.

Ignoring him, I kept my gaze locked on Karen. 'I didn't lie to you.'

'But you stretched the truth,' she accused with a choke of outrage. 'You don't care about me.'

'That's not true,' I protested.

'You want to save Jane and you want to use me to help you do it.'

'I just want your help identifying the man behind all this. If we get him, you can go back to your normal life.'

'Or I can die in the process!' she screamed, tears running down her face. She wasn't being rational, but that train had left the station a while ago when terror turned up to replace it.

Buck reached out to place a friendly hand on my shoulder. I shot an eyebrow in his direction which was enough to make him reconsider the move. I was done here though. Karen wasn't going to come with me tonight no matter what I said.

Making a point of letting my shoulders slump, I put my phone back into my jacket pocket and raised both hands in surrender.

'Karen, I am genuinely worried for you. I believe the police will grab this case and solve it, but I cannot wait for them to get up to speed. Jane can't wait,' I added, my voice quiet. 'I hope that you can. I want you to come with me so we can solve this together,' she sucked in a sharp breath to start arguing again, and I had to speak quickly to cut her off, 'but I can see that you are not going to.'

'No,' Karen confirmed. 'I am not. Like Buck said, it is time for you to leave now.'

I didn't move straight away. I wanted to ask her how she was going to feel when Jane's body was found and she could have helped us save her, but to do so would be both cruel and unfair. Instead, I asked, 'Can I send you some pictures? My team are working to identify the man. When they think they have him, will you tell me if he is the same man you saw in your bedroom?'

Karen Gilbert cast her eyes down, looking at the floor rather than meeting my eyes. After a second or so, she nodded her head; a small unhappy movement. 'Yes. I still don't think I will be able to identify him though.'

It was as good as I was going to get, and it was time to accept defeat.

Leaving the house with Hilary on my shoulder, I prayed Amanda was having better luck than me.

Aliases

FRIDAY, DECEMBER 23RD 1956HRS

Amanda

Jagjit hadn't found another one or, at least, he hadn't found another house owned by Toby Carter nearby to one of Jane's suspiciously missing women. What he had found was another example of two different houses owned by a man bearing the same name.

A little more trawling showed that Toby Carter only lived in the two houses under his name for a total of four years and three months and only eighteen months of that was in the first house.

The second name that cropped up twice was Alexander Banks. He lived in Sittingbourne near to a woman called Jennifer Metcalf in 1995 but moved away before she went missing and cropped up again in 2016 in the seaside resort of Sandwich. That's where a woman called Elise Dupont vanished. According to Land Registry he still owned the house.

We were onto something, I just didn't know what.

The file from Simon and Steven came with a picture. Apart from the name – Ramsey Mitchell - that was the only part I was interested in. The fifteen-year-old version of the man might look vastly different to the current model, but it was all I had to go on. His date of birth made him sixty-three today so he might have no hair or white hair or a wig. Glasses would change the angles of his face and his nose might have changed shape, been broken, or even have been subjected to surgery.

Until I found an up-to-date picture, I wouldn't know, and just like with Toby Carter, there were dozens of people out there by the same name.

While Jagjit continued to plug away at the neighbours' conundrum, I jumped into *LinkedIn* to search for each man, starting with Ramsey Mitchell since his fingerprints were on Jane's phone.

I got seventeen hits. Some were easy to dismiss because I was looking for a white guy in his sixties, but as I binned more and more of the options, a creeping sensation that he wasn't going to be there at all soon proved to be accurate.

Resetting, I searched for Toby Carter. This time I found thirteen Tobys and two hits that could be the right man. They were London based which wasn't so far away as to be unrealistic, and they looked more or less the right age. LinkedIn doesn't show ages which left me to guess how old each man might be. If, like everyone else, they used a good photograph and failed to update it ever, the pictures I was looking at could be at least five years old.

This was hardly an exact science.

I copied each picture and sent it to the printer, keeping the size small so the image wouldn't pixelate.

I met Alice there, 'I think I found someone,' she told me without sounding confident.

'We got a hit on the fingerprint,' I shared with her, handing her a copy of the email with the picture of the teenage Ramsey on.

'He looks like a criminal,' she commented.

It was an easy thing to say but rarely true. As a former police officer, I knew some of the biggest crooks wore suits. Besides, everyone looks guilty in their mug shots.

What I said was, 'Can you try to find him on social media? He doesn't show up on *LinkedIn*.'

'Not everyone does,' she pointed out.

That was true enough, but scrutinising the pictures I printed, I was still standing next to the printer when her images popped out.

'This is Toby Carter,' she held a picture up for me to see and my eyes almost popped out of my head. 'At least, it's the only Toby Carter the right age and race and stuff.'

Unthinkingly, I snatched the sheet of A4 from her hands, ran to the coffee table, and fell to my knees to place it side by side with the picture of Ramsey Mitchell as a teenager.

He had aged a lot over the prevailing five decades, but there was no way it wasn't the same person.

Alice leaned over my shoulder, a slight gasp escaping her lips when she saw the same thing that caught my attention. 'Is that the same person? Did he change his name?'

I shook my head. 'Maybe. Or he used aliases. A sudden thought jolted me. 'We need to get pictures of Alexander Banks!'

Getting Rubbed the Wrong Way

FRIDAY, DECEMBER 23RD 2001HRS

Tempest

I don't know how many times I have phoned Chief Inspector Ian Quinn, but whatever the number is, not one time has it been a pleasant experience. A few times in the past, we had come close to seeing eye to eye. We even attended a stag party together once. Well, not exactly together, but we were both there and managed to remain civil for the sake of the other attendees.

I tell myself that he is a good cop, someone who can be trusted, but the truth is I believe his self-interest threatens to overrule on doing what is decent a lot of the time. If he could snatch a victory from someone else and get away with it, he would do so. That applied doubly when it came to me, so it was with deep reservation that I placed a call to him now.

I knew he would answer it, just as I knew he would act like a dick and pretend I was wasting his time. He knew I wouldn't be calling him unless I needed something from him, and that I knew I wouldn't get what I needed unless I had something worthwhile to offer him.

'Mr Michaels,' his irritating voice filled my car.

'PC Jan Van Doorn has been taken by the Sandman.' I didn't bother with pleasantries.

I heard what might have been a grinding of his teeth before he replied. 'Is that supposed to jar me into motion, Mr Michaels?'

Staying calm, I said, 'One of your officers is in the hands of a serial killer, Quinn. If you fail to act, you will be held to account. I am recording this conversation, by the way,' I lied.

'I see. What evidence do you have to support your claim?'

I didn't have any. I was going off Big Ben's judgement call and he could be wrong. Were that the case though, I doubted very much he would be wrong about Jan being taken. It might not be the Sandman who had him, but given the convenience of the timing, I was willing to bet my shirt.

What I said was, 'Go to his apartment and check for yourself, Quinn. He is missing. His partner, Jane Butterworth, is missing, and we know the Sandman has Jane.' Feeling my ire rising, I changed tack so I could wrap the call up. 'Listen, Chief Inspector, I don't care which of us solves this crime, catches the bad guy, and gets the praise for it. I don't care one bit; there is no promotion in it for me.'

'You think that is what I care about?' he snapped in my ear.

'Ha! I know it is all you care about. Your public image is everything to you. So have the damned collar, I already said you could. But get your people moving and help me find Jane and Jan.'

He growled out his next words. 'Do not raise your voice

to me, Mr Michaels, I will not tolerate it. You sail too close to the wind all too often and seem to forget how generous I am with your misdemeanours.'

He kind of had a point. He knew I had been shooting a firearm in public yesterday and wouldn't have too much trouble proving it if he chose to. That was the subtextual threat I heard anyway.

Nevertheless, what I said next couldn't be printed. In the passenger seat, Hilary blushed.

Quinn was silent for a second, seething at the other end of the line. 'Any more of that, Mr Michaels, and I shall arrest you on sight the next time we meet. My team will investigate the alleged disappearance of Constable Van Doorn. If indeed he is missing, I will require a full statement from you.'

'I'll be at the Blue Moon office.' I said the words and jabbed the red button to end the call. Then I began the task of berating myself for losing my cool. I knew better than to raise my voice and use profanity. Generally, I pride myself on my ability to remain calm and unflustered when those around me are starting to panic.

There was something about Quinn that rubbed me the wrong way, I guess. He made me spit feathers more often than anyone I had ever met.

It was done now and even if I could undo it, I wasn't going to.

I pressed harder on the accelerator and fired the sleek, white Lotus toward the dark horizon. I was keen to get back to the office.

Electricity

FRIDAY, DECEMBER 23RD 2007HRS

Jane

It took another hour, using the heel of my boot to smash away at the plaster around the door until I exposed the electrics inside. There was no handle on the inside of the cell, nothing for me to grab and pull, and the gap around the door where it fitted into the frame was no greater than a fraction of an inch.

Once my hands were free and I could move on to tackle the door, I kicked it and shoved it and barged it with my shoulder just to see what it would do. All I got for my effort was some bruises. It was after I gave up kicking and shoulder barging it that I chose to attack the wall.

I surmised that there had to be a lock keeping the door closed. Maybe it was electronic and maybe it was mechanical. Maybe I could do like *Shawshank Redemption* and chip right through the wall to the other side.

I doubted there would be time for that, but luck chose to

give me a break because I found the cable almost straight away.

Well, actually, what I found was the plastic conduit it ran in, but its presence inside the wall made the plaster thin and when I whacked it, the conduit flexed a little and the plaster broke up.

It still took what felt like an hour and I found myself questioning how long I had been working at getting free. Was it three hours? Was it four? More than that? Where was the Sandman? Why wasn't he trying to stop me?

These questions and more swirled endlessly around my head as powder and grit from the plaster coated my skin. I was damp with sweat and deeply uncomfortable, but the option of taking a break never occurred to me. I was fighting for my life.

With almost a two-foot section of the conduit exposed, all the way from the mid-point of the door where I expected the lock to be, and upward to the top of the door almost, I started to yank at it.

It was not my first attempt to get the cable out of the wall, but previous attempts had all failed because I had too little leverage and too much of the conduit was still trapped inside the wall.

This time, losing a fingernail in the process, I was able to get enough purchase to rip it free.

By about an inch.

A fresh shower of plaster rained down to land at my stockinged feet. Sharp pieces were already digging in. My boots were ruined, the heels battered down to almost nothing, yet they were all I had and better for running and fighting in than forty denier nylon.

I shuffled carefully to the bed to put them back on, dusting off the soles of my feet as best I could first. Taking a second to eye up my latest challenge, it was time to see if I could convince the door to open.

As I said before, I am not an electrician. I can do stuff with computers but if you think those two things are somehow linked, you could not be more wrong. I never touch the electronics inside a computer; I simply manipulate the data available.

So looking at three wires as they exited the conduit to go into a device mounted inside the wall, I really had no idea what I was looking at. I also didn't have any tools, so stripping the wire, getting to the electricity inside and ... what? Hotwiring it? Not only did I have no idea how to do that, I also wasn't entirely sure what it meant.

I clenched my jaw, grabbed all the wires and the conduit, placed my right foot against the wall for leverage and ripped the whole lot from the device they fed.

Causing the wires to tear from their anchor points took only a fraction of the energy I applied, with the result that I flew backward, tripped, and slipped on the plaster detritus. I landed on the bed.

The door popped open with an audible click.

Listening

FRIDAY, DECEMBER 23RD 2011HRS

The Sandman

Listening intently to the sounds coming from Jane's cell, the Sandman stirred a small spoon around a China cup then set it delicately on the saucer. It was disappointing that he could not see her efforts; she was being thoroughly industrious if her grunting and straining were any indication.

Normally, by now he would have sung her to sleep, but using her as bait was keeping the Blue Moon team in the game. They had led him to Karen Gilbert already, but it was clear they knew too much so now he needed to ensure what they had discovered died with them.

His acolytes had a busy night ahead.

Once or twice, it had been necessary to postpone his gift and keep his chosen lady safe for the night in one of his purpose-built rooms. He liked when they tried to escape though, it was most entertaining to watch their endeavours. That was what he was doing now or would be if Jane hadn't found a way to black out the camera. None of the previous chosen had ever done that.

By the sounds of it, she was untied and trying to break out of the slumber room. It was an almost hopeless endeavour but not one he was going to attempt to stop. The more time she wasted the more tired she would be and thus the more she would welcome him singing her to sleep when the time came.

Soon he would travel to Harrietsham. Karen was waiting for him. His acolytes were already there, poised but awaiting his instructions. The finesse he would usually apply was no longer tenable and that irked him. However, the mission was more important than his personal desire for artistry.

Karen had to be saved.

Lost inside his own head, he jerked forward in his seat when he heard the door to Jane's room pop open. She'd been calling it a cell; a cruel term for what he regarded as a slumber zone. She, like all the others, could use the time to get some well-earned rest, yet he had come to accept that none ever would. They would fruitlessly try to escape the peace he promised them.

Sitting forward with keen anticipation, he saw Jane emerge from her room. The corridor outside was dimly lit – enough light for her to see by and enough for him to be able to see her delicate features and the emotions crossing her face.

A frown creased his forehead when he saw that she had not been crying. She was the first to ever escape the slumber zone, and she was the first to ever show such control over her fear. More often than not, when they awoke in the darkness, they curled into ball and sobbed until he came for them. Then they would beg and offer him things he didn't want.

Jane was doing neither thing, and appeared to have ripped a length of cable conduit from inside the wall. It wasn't much of a weapon, not wielded by a woman, but yet again, hefting a weapon was a behaviour he hadn't seen before.

Perplexed, he watched her begin to explore the corridor. Beneath ground, she would never find the way out, but she might find her boyfriend.

It was time to go, he decided, finishing his tea and placing the cup with its saucer to one side. Karen was more important. If Jane succeeded in rousing her boyfriend and freeing him from his slumber zone, they would face his acolytes and that would be the end of that.

Slipped Right Through Our Fingers

FRIDAY, DECEMBER 23RD 2024HRS

Amanda

Try as we might, we could not find pictures of Alexander Banks. There were men by that name, of course, and several different Alexandra Banks as well, which our search engine threw in for good measure. Having exhausted all the methods we could think of to find a picture of a man with that name who might match the photographs we already had, I took a moment to consider what it meant.

Voicing my thoughts to the room, I said, 'Toby Carter and Ramsey Mitchell are the same person. That much we can be sure of and I don't think many people, other than celebrities, have legitimate reasons for employing multiple aliases.'

Alice was about to say something when the sound of the office back door opening caught everyone's attention. The buzz of adrenalin hitting my bloodstream made my stomach tighten.

That was until I caught the heavenly salt and vinegar laden scent of fish and chips.

Big Ben burst through the inner door that leads to the back rooms and the carpark beyond. Hanging from one hand was a large white plastic bag, the contents of which could not be confused with anything else.

Basic strolled in behind him, another bag hanging from his right hand.

'Anyone hungry?' asked Big Ben with a grin. 'We have this bad habit of not stopping to eat and then suffering because of it. I don't know what's ahead, but we might as well face it with full bellies.'

I could pose no argument, the tightening in my stomach easing as it began to grumble its emptiness.

Rushing to clear a space on the coffee table, I told him, 'We found something.'

Big Ben put the bag down and shucked his outdoor jacket. 'Yeah?'

'Someone, actually, I should say.' I showed him the printed pictures of Toby Carter and Ramsey Mitchell.

While Big Ben scrutinised the two pieces of paper, one in each hand with his head going back and forth like a person watching tennis, Alice and Jagjit started to share out the fish suppers. Each paper parcel contained a large fillet of white fish deep-fried in a crispy batter and a large mound of unctuously soggy chips. The pungent smell of vinegar filled the air, making me glad it was after hours and no customers would be coming by.

'These are both the same person,' observed Big Ben, bringing the pictures into one hand so he could steal a chip with the other. 'This the guy then?'

'That's my current guess.' I shrugged. 'We haven't been able to come up with anything else. The print of his right index finger was on Jane's phone. I think that is a good enough indication. It's time to call the police, but I want to speak with Tempest before I do.'

As if remembering something he had omitted to tell me, Big Ben's food shovelling hand paused halfway to his mouth.

'I think Jan has been taken.'

The piece of fish I was eating almost fell out of my mouth and everyone else apart from Basic froze instantly.

'You don't think you should have led with that?' I questioned in shocked disbelief.

Big Ben rolled his eyes. 'I led with supper. Which, you know, you're welcome. You were showing me pictures and stuff. I only thought about it when you mentioned the police.'

I had my hands pressed against the sides of my face, grease from the fish and chips no doubt getting into my hair.

'Oh, my word. This is another level. I have to call the station. I have to get them involved now.' Though the idea made my stomach turn, I was going to have to get them to put me through to Chief Inspector Quinn. He and I hated each other, but this situation demanded I put my feelings aside and go high enough up the food chain to where I knew I would get a reaction.

'I think Tempest already called him,' said Big Ben around a mouthful of potato.

I yanked out my phone. 'Then I'm calling Tempest.'

Two seconds later, his voice was booming over the speaker so everyone in the room could hear it.

'Amanda, I hope you are doing better than me. I got nowhere with Karen. In fact, I probably made the situation worse though she has agreed to look at any pictures we want to send her. Oh, I think I went too far with Quinn as well. He's not going to help us no matter what we say.'

'Did you tell him about Jan Van Doorn?' I blurted quickly before Tempest could say anything else.

I could hear the irritation in Tempest's voice when he said, 'I did. He did his usual thing of acting like I must be making it up, but I could tell he believed me. He's probably got officers at his apartment right now. Is Ben back?'

'I am,' answered Big Ben. 'I bought fish 'n' chips. If you hurry, there might be some left.'

'Ooh, fish and chips,' repeated Hilary excitedly. 'I'm starving.'

I cut over the men and their stomachs. 'Tempest, I think I found him. The Sandman I mean. There was a fingerprint on Jane's phone, and it matches a person who lived next door to one of the victims a while ago.' I held my phone over the picture of Toby Carter and pressed the button to take a photograph. 'I'm sending you a shot now. The quality might not come through great.'

Tempest fell silent, waiting for his phone to ping with the incoming message. We all knew when it did because the phone exploded with expletives.

Cautiously, I asked, 'Tempest?'

He swore again, then said, 'I'm fine. You're right. That's the Sandman. There's no need to ask Karen.'

Big Ben frowned. 'How can you be so sure?'

Tempest's words came back with a tone of dreadful finality to them. 'Because I was talking to him earlier. That's Karen Gilbert's next-door neighbour. His name is Harry Hengist.'

Time for Action

FRIDAY, DECEMBER 23RD 2031HRS

Tempest

The face on the picture Amanda sent me bore a wry smile. To me, it seemed like I was being mocked. I'd had him pressed into the carpet and completely in my control, yet he played me like a fiddle.

Hilary said, 'He knew who you were the whole time.'

I could feel my back teeth clenching together. The memory of Harry Hengist's wide eyes when he opened the door made sense now. He was at home and he knew who I was. He must have thought I had worked it all out and was there to bust him.

I wasn't though, I was just an idiot knocking on doors and asking questions. Once he saw my guileless expression, he visibly relaxed. Why wouldn't he? I told him everything he wanted to know about how my investigation was going.

I cursed loudly and tried to crush the steering wheel with my grip. I felt like driving straight to his house and dragging him out by his tongue. I wouldn't bother to knock this time either. I was in the mood to drive my car right through the front door.

However, the situation called for an emotionless, controlled response. One that involved back up and redundancy to ensure he could not escape. What troubled me most was the distinct possibility Jane was in his house the whole time I was there. Did it have a basement? I never did find out.

I didn't know the answer to that question and my gut reaction was that style of house did not include a floor below ground. How hard would it be for a person to dig one though? Maybe it was in the garden. A few decades ago, citizens of Kent were digging Anderson shelters to hide in when the Germans dropped bombs on the county like it was confetti. Harry's house could still have one for all I knew.

Jane might even have been locked in a soundproof room in the house. She might have been unconscious or tied up. I just didn't know, but I was going hell for leather to find out now.

I had to slow my speed as I came into Rochester. I broke a hundred on the motorway and came screaming down the hill toward the city until I started hitting traffic. There was something going on at the castle, the streets filled with pedestrians dressed in Victorian garb. It would be another Dickens thing, possibly an outdoor play.

I didn't care what it was, but I did care that I had to slow down to a crawl to get through it. I honked my horn angrily until I saw children among the revellers. It was Christmas Eve in a few hours and here I was playing the part of Scrooge or the Grinch.

Suffering silently, I got through the press of people and to my office just along from the cathedral. The car door didn't shut as I ran at the office rear door and I didn't care. I was going back out soon enough.

I burst through the final door that led me into the main office space to find Big Ben already suiting up. Basic was too, and Amanda. Only Jagjit and Alice were still wearing their normal clothes but then they both knew I wouldn't want them to get involved in a task such as this one.

Some days it feels like I have been a paranormal investigator for half my life, yet I opened the firm in the spring of this year. We haven't yet reached our one-year anniversary but looking around at my friends, I had to take stock of all that had occurred in those few months.

That three of my friends, including my girlfriend were donning black combat gear and getting ready to storm the house of a maniac ought to give me pause to consider my life choices. Did I ever really have a choice though?

I didn't choose to be a paranormal investigator, and I most certainly didn't choose to take on a serial killer who likes to kidnap women and murder them while he sings them to sleep. The choices were not mine, but the decision to deal with the consequences of my situation were.

I could go home, open a beer, and cuddle up with Amanda and the dogs on the couch. Except, I couldn't. Not really. Duty and responsibility demanded I take direct action and try to save Jane.

Was she still alive? I had no idea, but when Big Ben handed me my own set of body armour, I knew I would find out soon enough.

'Back to New Ash Green?' asked Amanda as I took off my jacket and started fastening the Kevlar vest over my normal clothes.

I nodded, tugging on the Velcro to secure my armour in place. 'We should take two cars even though we could all fit in Big Ben's. The last thing we want is to break down or have something else happen to delay us.' I told them about my encounter with Harry Hengist earlier.

Jagjit jogged over to the desk in my office, settling into my chair. 'Can you spell that?'

I had no idea why he wanted the name but just as I was starting to draw out the plan of the house – what little I had seen of it – Jagjit called out that he had no hits for Harry Hengist other than the house he currently occupied.

'He might also have a house in Sandwich,' Amanda told me. 'Could he have gone there? We found that one under a different name, but I think it is safe to assume he lived near many if not all of his victims.'

I pursed my lips and shook my head. 'My gut says he is staying in New Ash Green. The place looked lived in. The lawn had been mowed; the garden was tidy. There were shoes stacked underneath the coat rack. If he took Jane and Jan, unless he took them in the same trip, he must be operating closer than Sandwich. There and back twice is too far to go for him to then be in New Ash Green for me to find him at home. He had no idea I was going to turn up at his house so why would he be there if Jane and Jan are somewhere else?'

'Those are valid points,' Amanda conceded. 'You know raiding his house is highly illegal, right?'

I gritted my teeth. 'I don't care. I will gladly do a spell in jail just to get this guy.'

'Me too,' Big Ben threw his hat in the ring. 'We don't get up to nearly enough illegal stuff anyway.'

I wasn't sure what he meant – we were always doing things we knew might get us in hot water. Now was not the time for a discussion though. Now was the time to open the box of weapons we kept in the corner of the storage room.

Before we went there, I slowly spun on the spot, making eye contact with everyone one at a time.

'No one has to come along on this venture. Big Ben and I are the ones trained for this.'

'Oh, shut up, Tempest,' snapped Amanda. 'I'm the former police officer. You were trained to shoot people and blow stuff up. Raiding houses is my territory, not yours.'

'Okay,' I conceded and turned to look at Basic. 'Basic this could get you into a lot of trouble. If they lock you up there will be no one to look after your mum. You really don't have to come.'

I was often reluctant to involve Basic for the simple reason that I wasn't sure he even knew what was going on half the time. If he ended up in jail, there would be consequences beyond the impact on him as an individual. However, his response made it clear he had thought about that already.

In a surprising burst of eloquence, he shrugged and said, 'It's not always easy having friends. If it were, you wouldn't really know if dem people were friends or not. Besides, I hired a nurse for mum already.'

That he had strung a sentence together stunned all of us into silence until Jagjit spoke. 'We can come too. If you need the numbers.'

I shook my head firmly and gripped his shoulder in a comradely fashion to show my thanks.

'Amanda is right that we are about to break a bunch of laws. You should go home, open a bottle of something cold, and pretend you were never involved.'

'Unless we get away with it,' added Big Ben. 'Then you'll want to get your faces in the paper like the rest of us.' He held up one hand and ran it through the air as if outlining a headline when he said, 'Local Adonis saves

Christmas from maniac. Small, less attractive people helped.'

Amanda smacked him in the groin. As he groaned and folded slightly at the waist, I started toward the storeroom in the back where we kept the weapons and the radios. It was time to get kitted up.

No Need for Stealth

FRIDAY, DECEMBER 23RD 2109HRS

Tempest

No one said much on the drive to New Ash Green. Partly that was nerves stopping us from chattering – I greeted my anxiety like an old friend, it would help to keep me sharp. The other reason we remained quiet was because there just wasn't anything to say.

We had been over the plan, what there was of it, and accepted we were going to have to make it up as we went along.

Harry Hengist, or whatever his real name is, would be home or he wouldn't. Jane and Jan would be there, or they wouldn't, and they were either still alive or they were not. It was a grim business and no mistake.

Would the Sandman have weapons? Would there be booby traps in his house? What horrors would we face?

I suspected we were all ... well, maybe not Basic, but the rest of us were for sure running the different unknowns through our heads and that was keeping us quiet too.

I was in the Lotus with Amanda. Big Ben was following behind in his giant utility truck thing. A lot of the journey was through the Kent countryside, passing through small villages and constantly slowing down, yet we reached our destination in under thirty minutes.

It was getting cold out, our breath forming clouds of vapour above our heads once we left the warmth of the cars. Not that Big Ben's was all that warm with a missing window.

Choosing to park down the street so our arrival would not be so obvious, Basic and Amanda were going around the back, jumping fences and fighting through overgrown alleyways. Big Ben and I were going in through the front.

We would knock first; it was the sensible thing to do. Assuming the Sandman couldn't see who was outside, he might just open the door. It was easier than kicking it in which, for some reason, Big Ben seemed reluctant to try.

Harry Hengist didn't answer the door which came as no surprise, so we moved to full assault mode. Using my radio, I checked on Amanda and Basic.

'We're going in – forced entry. Any sign of movement at the back of the house?'

Amanda's voice crackled over the airwaves. 'No. The house looks dead. No sign of life at all.'

'Is there a shed or something in the garden where he might have them stashed?'

'Nothing that I can see. There is no sound either. It's so quiet here I can tell what the people next door are watching on their TV.'

I let her know we were going in the next two seconds then jumped out of my skin as the bay window at the front of the house exploded.

'What was that?' blurted Amanda, her voice instantly filled with concern.

I was looking at what it was but struggling to believe it.

'Um, Ben just made an entry point,' I told her, uncertain how else I could describe it.

Big Ben was looking pleased with himself. 'Much easier than kicking in a door,' he commented as he pulled the large wooden picnic bench back out through the hole he made.

'Where did you even find it?' I had to know.

He threw the picnic bench to one side and jerked a thumb over his shoulder. 'It was in a garden across the street.' Before I could say anything else, he cleared away the broken glass and hopped inside.

So much for stealth.

I clambered in after him, whispering into my radio, 'Stand by, we are in the house.'

We moved swiftly, both carrying blunt weapons to be used only if necessary and checking what lay beyond each doorway before we stepped through it. There was no way anyone in the house could be oblivious to our entry and that meant the Sandman would be on high alert if he was here.

Thus, the need for stealthy movement was largely eroded and swiftness became our ally.

It took seconds to check the ground floor of the house: kitchen, dining room, downstairs cloakroom, and living room, the last of which was now full of cold air and bits of glass. There was nothing to find and no sign that a serial killer lived here. Bookshelves contained books and a pile of neatly stacked mail lay beneath a small paperweight on a desk. Pans used for dinner were balanced on the drying rack next to the sink. It all looked so innocent and normal.

There was no door leading to a set of stairs down to a

basement that we could find, and we were diligent enough to check the bookshelves to make sure they didn't hide secret compartments.

Big Ben ran up the stairs, throwing caution to the wind as he exposed himself to an attack he would not see coming until it was too late.

No attack came and once we were upstairs, I knew our target wasn't here, and neither were Jane and Jan. My heart was sinking, the terrible knowledge that I had him in my grasp a few short hours ago burning into my conscience like a red-hot brand.

'There's someone out here!' Amanda's sudden shout sent a jolt of electricity through me.

I threw myself at the stairs, getting there just before Big Ben as we both clutched at the vague hope we could still find our friends and avert disaster.

Our haste proved counterproductive. In the darkness, I failed to see an object on the stairs. When my lead foot found it, I slipped and fell, pitching forward and grabbing wildly for the banister.

I would have managed to save myself from falling all the way, but Big Ben was right on my heels and moving too fast to stop. Just as I arrested my fall, he piled into me and we both fell, spinning in the air as we sailed the last yards to land in a painful heap in the hallway below.

There being no time to account for our injuries, we got in each other's way yet again as we both scrambled to get up and get moving.

With a shout of frustrated rage, we burst from the rear of the house, two black-clad warriors ready to hand out a beating to anyone available.

'What are you two clowns doing?' asked Amanda, appearing from the shadow under a tree. 'It sounded like elephants learning to tango in there. I thought you were going to be stealthy.'

Looking around for the source of danger, my senses on high alert, I asked, 'Where is he?'

'Who? Oh, yeah, that was a cat. Sorry.' I could see Amanda's embarrassed grin in the moonlight.

'A cat?' questioned Big Ben, out of breath and nursing his shoulder where he probably bruised it falling down the stairs.

'I take it there's no one inside,' Amanda went around me to enter the house.

I paused for a second, scanning the back garden but there was no shed in which Harry might have stashed Jane and Jan. Wherever they were, they were not here.

Amanda touched my arm. 'Come on. We need to look for clues inside and the chances are the police are already on their way.'

Not Alone

FRIDAY, DECEMBER 23RD 2112HRS

Jane

It had been light inside my cell but the hallway beyond was dark. Starkly so after the bright white walls my eyes were now used to. It felt good to be free of the cell, yet really all I had done was conquer one more obstacle. How many more were there before I could be free? If I knew that, I might have cause to rejoice.

Leaving my cell door open cast light into the darkness beyond and created shadows too. The corridor was bare brick – large grey breeze blocks I could smash through if I had a few tools. It was four feet wide and came to a dead end just to the left of my cell door. Turning right led into the darkness as the corridor stretched out before me.

I went that way, doing my best to walk in my boots now that both heels were broken. Three yards later the light from my cell was fading fast, the blackness eating more of it the farther I went. I pushed on, telling my eyes to hurry up to adjust. When I came to a door to my right, I stopped.

On the same side of the wall as my cell, was another one. The door was exactly like the one to my cell. When I looked, I could see at least one more on the same wall just a few yards farther along. Examining the first one, I poked it to confirm it would not swing open and tried the handle.

The handle refused to turn – it was electronically locked just like mine. Was it another cell? The door looked the same, it was locked, and it was located in the same creepy underground bunker.

Underground.

I hadn't thought about it before, but now I was free of my cell, the air was laden with a damp mustiness I associated with old cellars. I was below ground. Would that make it harder for anyone to find me? Where the heck was I for that matter?

My thoughts that maybe the Sandman had me in a room beneath his house could still be correct but if so, he had a big house. The dimensions of the area I was in would not fit beneath a standard semi-detached place and had to be three times the footprint of a terraced house. And that was just the bit I could see.

When a noise came from the other side of the cell door, I leapt backward in fright. So unexpected was it that I almost lost control of my bladder and came to rest with my back pressed against the opposite wall.

With my pulse banging in my ears, I could barely hear the sound but when it came a second time, I realised I was listening to a person. They were trying to make themselves heard through a gag, the words coming out as unintelligible mumbles.

I rushed back to the door, placing my ear right up to the edge where it met the frame. 'Hello?' I called into the dark.

There was a moment of silence before the person on the

other side said, 'Ayne?' I couldn't make out what he was trying to say – it was definitely a man – yet the noise he made sounded hopeful and excited.

'Hello,' I tried again. 'Are you trapped in there? I just managed to get out of my cell. I was trapped next door. Can you hear me? Can you get your gag off?'

'Owww!' complained a voice that made my heart jump.

I squealed, 'Jan!' My boyfriend was behind the door. Trapped in a cell in an underground space just like me. It should not give me comfort to discover he was a captive too, but it did. I wasn't alone, and even though that meant he wasn't out there looking for me, it meant a lot to have him here. He was making spitting noises as if trying to get something out of his mouth. I remembered the ball of cotton wool.

'Yeah,' he replied after a second. 'Yeah, it's me. Are you okay?'

'The Sandman has us!' I blurted somewhat redundantly.

From the other side of the cold steel door, Jan said, 'That would be my guess. I didn't know he had helpers.'

'Helpers?'

'Six guys dressed like weird cult members came into my apartment just after I got home from my shift. I tried to fight them but ... well, one of them had a needle. The last thing I remember is the sting as it went into my neck. If the Sandman has us, then he has a bunch of henchmen working for him.'

This was unwelcome news. Until I heard it, I was operating under the belief that once free, I would only have to fight the Sandman, a man who I believed to be close to retirement age. My likelihood of success might not have been high before, but it was markedly less so now.

Jan broke my train of thought by asking a question,

'How did you get out? You said you were in a cell. I guess I am too, but there is no light in here. I can't see a thing.'

'It wasn't easy,' I admitted with a sorrowful sigh. 'Are you tied up?'

Jan huffed. 'Yes. My hands are behind my back. Getting the damned gag off was hard enough. I managed to rip my right ear which is now bleeding. How on Earth did you get out of your ropes?'

It had taken me hours to get free and now we needed to do the same thing with Jan. Would there be something in his room that he could use to saw through the rope like I had? We were going to have to find out.

I crouched to see if there was a gap under the door. Maybe I could find something down here he could use to cut his ropes.

However, Jan claimed no light was coming under the door, so the gap, if there was one, was too narrow for anything worthwhile to go through.

Leaning against the wall, I began to explain all the things I had done to get free.

Time to go!

FRIDAY, DECEMBER 23RD 2120HRS

Tempest

Tossing the house as swiftly as we could, the four of us split up to attack different rooms. Amanda and Big Ben went upstairs, rifling through drawers and closets. Basic got the kitchen which left me the living room with its trashed window plus the dining room/study.

We had to be swift. The likelihood that the police were coming too high to hang about. However, being swift increased the probability that we would miss whatever there was to find here.

The desk yielded nothing of interest. On it was a plan of some woodland, but in the two seconds I spent studying it, I found nothing to suggest it was of any interest. I checked underneath it to be sure it didn't hide a glaringly obvious clue to the Sandman's location. Then a thought occurred to me and I ran to the front door to look for keys.

That he had another property somewhere was obvious

The Sandman

now and of no surprise. I was also convinced that it would be local which is to say I expected it to be within the county.

Kent is not a small county.

The key hooks contained bunches for a car, a few odd keys that might open anything and a large ring with a single key for a large padlock. I pocketed the lot.

Amanda appeared at the top of the stairs. 'Tempest, I've found something.'

I ran up them two at a time, watching for the thing I tripped over earlier. At the top, I followed her into the master bedroom where she handed me a framed photograph.

It was of an attractive woman in her twenties. Her hairstyle and clothes were from the eighties, but filing that information away, the thing that stood out most was how much like Karen Gilbert she looked.

'I think it's his wife,' Amanda whispered.

It made perfect sense. Or it might if you are a psycho serial killer.

Whipping out my phone, I dialled Jagjit.

He answered on the first ring. 'Hey, Tempest. I didn't expect to hear from you so soon. Did you get him already?'

I sucked a little air through my teeth. 'No. It's a total bust. He's not here and neither is Jane. Listen, I need you to check something out for me.'

'Sure. Go for it.'

Between Amanda and me, we steered him to research the fake names we found for Harry Hengist – the one on his arrest sheet was almost certainly the real one. Did that man marry? What happened to his wife? Was she still alive? Was she the first victim?

Amanda studied the psychology of serial killers at university, using her knowledge now to explain to Jagjit how serial killers are usually recreating a moment from their past when they kill. Or attempting to relive an experience that traumatised them so they can re-enact it the way they wanted it to have been. That the Sandman's killing spree may have started with his wife sounded highly likely.

Big Ben called to get our attention.

I wished Jagjit good luck and followed Amanda from the room.

Big Ben was in the attic, his face looking back down through the hole in the ceiling. A telescopic ladder hung down to the landing below.

'You're not going to believe this,' he claimed.

Amanda went up first, a gasp of surprise coming the moment she stuck her head through the hole. I raced up after her, my eyes swinging around to take it all in.

Unlike most attics across the planet, which house suitcases, old bits of furniture and things the kids have grown out of, but the grandkids might want, the Sandman's attic was a shrine to all the women he had murdered.

The clutter was there too but pushed into the corners. There were photographs, far more than we expected and yet again, every woman bore similar hair and facial features. He was selecting them because they looked like his wife. That was the conclusion my brain wanted to draw. Each photograph was of a woman arranged the same way River Tam had been. I spotted her too. The shot was taken at a different angle from the one I'd seen before; this one getting taken by the man responsible for her death.

Big Ben tapped a box with his hand. 'There are mementos too,' he revealed.

A siren in the distance broke the spell before I could decide I was curious enough to explore further. We had to go and there was no time left for anything.

Charging down the stairs yet again, I shouted, 'Basic! We are leaving!'

He appeared from the kitchen with a peanut butter sandwich in his hands. 'I found a sandwich,' he mumbled around the gob of bread in his mouth.

I grabbed his arm and ran for the front door, towing him along behind me.

Getting caught now was not part of the plan.

Amanda and Big Ben hit the bottom of the stairs, all four of us flying from the house, though only one had a sandwich hanging from their mouth as we ran across the driveway and back to the road.

The siren wasn't alone. There were several of them, but they were all coming from one direction.

The keys in my pocket jangled, making a terrible racket until I crushed them against my body. The cars were just along the street parked nose to tail one behind the other with the Lotus nearest to us.

We split up again, Amanda diving into my car as Big Ben plipped his truck open for him and Basic. Engines roared and we set off, pulling away fast to get some distance between us and the approaching police.

If we could get out of the street, the police would arrive and find only a suspicious mess where we had been. We were all wearing gloves so there would be only minimal evidence to tie us to the scene and since I had been there earlier today, I could argue any trace fibres from Amanda, Big Ben, or Basic could have transferred from my clothing.

Breaking into a serial killer's home to prove that's what he was could be easily justified, especially on the hunt for two missing persons. Yet explaining all this to the police would eat up time that we didn't have.

We knew for certain that Harry Hengist/Ramsey

Mitchell or whatever name showed up on his passport was the Sandman, and we had led the police to his house. Quinn wouldn't be able to ignore the case now though I felt sure he was already investigating it after our most recent chat.

I glanced in my rear-view mirror as I reached the end of the road. Behind me, the flashing lights of approaching police cars were bouncing off the buildings, but they were yet to turn into the same street we were on.

We were going to make it.

Making a fast left turn, I rounded the corner, watched Big Ben follow me and allowed myself to relax.

Until Amanda swore.

Too busy checking behind, I hadn't paid attention to what was in front of me. As my eyes twitched across to see what had startled Amanda, I saw it too.

Fifty yards ahead, parked side on so it blocked the road, a squad car with its lights off sat waiting for us.

Unable to go forward, I hit the brakes. I could back up and go a different way but that would be running from the police and was not a policy I could endorse. It would only make matters worse.

Then Chief Inspector Quinn got out of the squad car and I realised that things were already about as bad as they could get.

Busted

FRIDAY, DECEMBER 23RD 2122HRS

Tempest

We all got to watch as Quinn stepped from the car and spoke into his radio. The squad cars we were trying to evade didn't stop at the house next to Karen Gilbert's. They kept coming, reaching the end of the road where they formed a blockade behind us.

We weren't trying to run. Not anymore. Like I said, it would only make matters worse.

They were not squad cars as I expected though, it was a full tactical unit – armed officers approaching us as if we were dangerous terrorists.

'Don't move,' hissed Amanda, gripping my left thigh across the seats. 'If they get twitchy, they will shoot.'

I knew she was right. Tragic incidents had made the news headlines in the past. The officers, their level of alertness and preparedness to react heightened, would shoot first if they felt their target was going to draw a weapon. Afterward, an enquiry would determine whether the officers were right to fire, but the victim would be just as dead no matter the outcome.

I checked my rear-view, reassuring myself that Big Ben wasn't going to do anything stupid. His hands were raised, palms open to show the officers they were empty. Amanda and I did the same.

Using hand gestures, Quinn drew the officers from their cars and sent them in our direction. They rushed us, crowding the cars with their weapons pointed at our heads. Most held back, watching us for danger as if daring us to make a foolish move while others darted in to rip the doors open.

Orders were barked, raised voices commanding us to keep our hands in sight and exit the cars.

Rough hands pulled us to the ground.

'Quinn!' I bellowed. 'Stop this! We know who the Sandman is. Help us to find him!'

I could hear Amanda on the other side of the car being handled every bit as roughly as me. Twisting my head around, I could also see Big Ben. He was on his chest with cuffs being snapped on his wrists. Ever the clown, he shot me a grin and made his eyes go crossed.

This was no laughing matter though. Quinn was doing exactly what I expected him to. He could see a potential win and he was going to make sure he got it. All he had to do was make sure I was out of the way and illegally breaking into the Sandman's house handed him the means to do it.

Trying again as they hauled me to my feet, I shouted, 'Quinn. The clock is ticking. You must let us help you! Lives are at stake.'

Up to that point, Quinn had not deemed us worthy of addressing, but my latest rage-filled rant changed that.

'Help?' he repeated. 'You continue to delude yourself

The Sandman

that you are helping.' The officer holding my right bicep in a vice-like grip wheeled me around until I was facing his boss.

Quinn was coming my way, making a beeline for me as his driver shifted the squad car to unblock the road.

His tone was passive aggressive and yet also borderline bored. 'You broke into a house, destroying the front façade if my officers there are to be believed. Doing so compromised the chain of evidence and will fuel the defence lawyers with get-out clauses since they can argue you planted anything we find. What you have done is criminal, Mr Michaels, and this time you are going to be charged.'

I was seething. 'How swiftly would you have found that house had I not shoved this case down your throat, Quinn? I have led you every inch of the way. Earlier today you denied the possibility that the Sandman even existed. Now you want to blame me for ruining evidence you wouldn't have known to look for?'

Dismissively, Quinn turned his back, nodding his head at the sergeant leading the armed unit.

'Take them away. I'll interview them myself later.'

And that was it. The police had a van waiting for us, and we were going to be locked up for the night.

At Quinn's retreating head, I shouted, 'Jane is out there right now! He has her, Quinn. He has her and he is going to kill her. Tell me you are going to throw everything at this, Quinn!'

I got no answer, he didn't even bother to acknowledge that he had heard me.

A hand cupped the top of my head as I was pushed into the van.

'Mind your head,' advised the officer, loading me in next to Amanda. Big Ben and Basic were on the other side, facing us. Their faces were emotionless, unlike mine which couldn't decide what it wanted to do. I was madder than a box of wasps and it was a good thing I was cuffed because I would have punched Quinn in the face if my hands were free. More than my anger though was the sense of despair.

Ultimately, we had failed. I had failed. Whatever was going to happen to Jane was going to happen now and there was nothing I could do about it. Jan would likely share the same fate. Would their bodies ever be found? Jane identified so many missing women and after seeing the Sandman's attic, we knew there were even more. The police would do a full count and match photographs to missing women, but how was it they all stayed missing? Jane's report showed us pictures of River Tam, a young woman found lovingly arranged just like the ones in the attic. So why had she been found but none of the rest ever had? How was it that this man continued to kill and never got caught?

As it turned out, I had the whole night to consider those questions.

A Noise in the Dark

FRIDAY, DECEMBER 24TH 0215HRS

Jane

I was bone tired and now that I wasn't doing much moving, I was also getting cold. My clothes were damp with perspiration from the extreme effort of getting myself free and that was ruining the thermal insulation properties they might have offered.

My hands, shoulders, forearms, and above all, my abs hurt still but the pain had receded to be nothing more than a dull ache. I would hurt worse tomorrow (if I lived that long), and I fervently hoped to experience it.

With me giving him encouragement through the door, Jan was fighting to get free of his bindings, but he was having far less luck than me and the lack of light in his cell was not helping.

After what had to be about four hours of effort, he was still working on the bindings around his feet. He got his hands around to the front of his body but succeeded in popping his shoulder out of its socket to do so. He and I both suspected it was dislocated, the pain from it encumbering his efforts further.

Neither he nor I had any idea what the time might be. He arrived home at close to four this afternoon and was grabbed minutes later. It had to be after midnight now I felt sure, but in the dark, and with no way to track the passage of time, it could be morning or afternoon or ... well, you get the picture.

'How's it going?' I asked for maybe the fiftieth time.

I'd been listening to him pant and struggle for a while and remembered how exhausting I found the task. Having arrived home in his uniform, he had copper's boots on still so unlike my ankles, where the Sandman foolishly tied the ropes around my boots to leave me wiggle room, Jan's ropes were above the boots and wriggling did nothing but chafe his skin. He'd taken the boots off, but it made little difference to the task.

With a gasp to get his breath back before speaking, Jan said, 'I just can't get the ropes on my legs to shift. I've switched to work on my wrists. The duct tape is coming away slowly, but I can't find the end so I'm having to gnaw through it.'

I could only imagine how tough the task was in the dark. It had been hard enough for me and I could see what I was doing. A yawn split my face. Lasting for seconds, I started to feel like I might be asleep before it stopped.

I was desperate to lie my head down and just get a little nap. I even had an argument raging in my head because getting some sleep might be the best thing I could do.

Just as I considered that Jan would be able to wake me easily enough if he needed to, I heard a noise coming from above. It was the first time there had been any sound since I first arrived. It jolted me, sending ice through my veins and cramps to my core. Jan froze too, all sounds of his struggle stopping abruptly.

Someone was coming.

Everything According to his Plan

SATURDAY, DECEMBER 24TH 0217HRS

Ramsey Mitchell

Taking Karen Gilbert had been easy enough. Tempest Michaels led them straight to her just as he hoped. Soon she would sleep but it was too late now to perform the ceremony this night. If he were to sing her to sleep, it would have to wait until the sun set again.

That it was now Christmas Eve mattered not one bit. If anything, the timing was more perfect for it. His acolytes were feverish with excitement at the prospect of *saving* three new lives. He would attend to Karen himself but had decided to reward his senior circle with the honour of bestowing graceful slumber on the other two.

In so doing, he would, in a sense, elevate those involved and cause those who were not yet deemed worthy to clamour ever more for his favour. They would work harder than ever.

Besides, Jane Butterworth did not resemble his precious Valerie and as for the young police officer, well ... he had to die simply because he was involved. Taken as a precaution to make Jane comply in case Tempest did not lead him to Karen Gilbert, his kidnap ultimately proved unnecessary. Such is the nature of taking precautions – one can never tell what issues may or may not arise.

Pausing at the door that led to the cells, he cleared his throat to get everyone's attention.

'Gentlemen, when we open the door, we must take care not to harm our guest. She has escaped from her cell and may be in a state of agitation.' A ripple of murmurs passed through his followers. 'Yes, yes, I know. She ought to have accepted the grace of our blessing and remained in her slumber room. Please take care to treat her gently and be prepared for her to attempt a physical assault.'

A voice asked, 'Do we subdue her, master?'

'Yes, but do so gently. We wish her no harm remember. I will administer the sleep serum myself.' Mitchell tapped his pocket to confirm his bottle of etorphine was still there before saying, 'Open the door.'

The lights inside the basement flickered on as they came in, the Sandman using the sudden harsh white light to blind Jane and disorient her. His acolytes swarmed in, all bar the two carrying Karen Gilbert's limp form.

Walking with calm strides as his men rushed forward, Mitchell got to watch as Jane flailed and fought. She was strong for a woman, he observed, and appeared to have been given some fight training.

Though blinking against the light and attempting to shield her eyes, she lanced out a fist that connected with a chin. One of his acolytes jerked backward from the blow and another caught a swinging foot somewhere he really didn't want it. The outrushing whoosh of air sufficient to let everyone know the blow found its target.

Inevitably, that was all she got before the volume of arms and hands pinned her to a wall. She squealed in terror and anger, thrashing violently as he approached, the bottle of etorphine in one hand and a syringe in the other.

Foul language spat from her lips, and her boyfriend, still trapped in his cell bellowed his outrage too.

Soothingly, he reached out his left hand to stroke her blonde hair. 'It will all be over soon, Jane. You have served your purpose well.' Mitchell stepped to his left, providing a clear view down the corridor where Karen Gilbert hung between two of his men. 'Look who we have brought to celebrate with you.'

'No.' The word slipped from between Jane's lips like a moan of denial. It acted like the last straw, the tall, thin woman sagging between her captors as the fight went from her.

A short while later, all three of his honourees were securely back in the slumber rooms where they could rest until it was time for their ascension. All were drugged and would remain so for many hours, but as Ramsey Mitchell walked away, intent on dealing with the Blue Moon team, there were several things he didn't know.

One of those things was the object Jane had tucked in her boot.

Learning from a Master

SATURDAY, DECEMBER 24TH 1127HRS

Quinn

'This is good work, Ian. Well done.'

'Thank you, sir.'

'Terrible business in Harrietsham though,'

Chief Inspector Quinn's lips twitched in annoyance. 'Yes, sir.' The chief constable for Kent had visited him in person, a sure sign that he saw political gain in being associated with the successful conclusion of the Sandman case. Quinn chose to use the name Tempest Michaels coined and sell it as his own. Now that he'd seen the evidence, including that which he'd confiscated from the Blue Moon office, he knew the press would see why it was such a good name for the serial killer *he'd* discovered, and they would love it.

There was a certain catchiness to the name that would capture headlines and the public's imagination.

Karen Gilbert being taken was not part of the plan though.

'You're certain it is the work of this so-called Sandman?' Chief Constable Vickery wanted to know.

Quinn had already assured the man it was, but if the big boss wanted him to say it again, he would. The promotion board's next meeting was right around the corner after all.

'Yes, sir. She was victimised by Ramsey Mitchell, a man we now know to have more than a dozen aliases. My team were able to establish a pattern of behaviour that saw him purchase properties close to each of his victims. Sometimes, as was the case with Miss Gilbert, he was able to buy the house next door. At this time, we are unsure what his motivation for the murders might be, but we believe he has been killing since 1984 with at least one victim each year.

The chief constable's eyebrows shot to the sky. 'How did he go undetected for so long, man?'

Quinn skewed his lips to one side before answering. It gave him time to think about how likely it was that his own failings might be discovered. Several of the missing women had passed through his hands as cases he dismissed. A missing woman was not a murder and therefore not headline news. He wanted cases he could solve, not open-ended messes that would tarnish his amazing record.

Knowing his boss was waiting for an answer, he said, 'I believe he was able to ensure we never found the bodies.'

Chief Constable Vickery challenged his answer instantly. 'What about River Tam?' His eyes were narrowed at his subordinate. He'd heard about Quinn and knew the man's father when he served. He'd been an ambitious man and the son seemed no different. There was nothing wrong with that; he hadn't risen to be chief constable by failing to take advantage of the chances when they arose. However, if Quinn was trying to pull the wool over his eyes, he was going to find his ambitions halted sharply.

'Yes, sir. I believe River Tam to be the outlier. You will recall, no doubt, that the investigation into her murder was conducted by Chief Constable Beattie. I believe he did a stalwart job,' Quinn added quickly in case his boss thought he was trying to deflect. 'I'm certain I could have done no better,' an outright lie, 'and, of course, there were no other bodies to suggest this was a serial killer. I believe the other bodies are most likely buried, sir. River Tam was found by a farmer not long after she was murdered. I believe it will be proven that Ramsey Mitchell was disturbed before he could inter her body.'

The chief constable pursed his lips and considered Quinn's explanation.

'Perhaps. Listen Quinn. It's good work, like I said, but there is no time to rest. One of your officers is missing still and now Miss Gilbert. The press have got hold of it already and I have to face them shortly. I'll be assuring them we are doing everything we can to catch this blighter, and you are going to make sure that is true.'

Listening to hear what else the chief constable might have to say, Quinn suddenly realised his boss was waiting for him to agree. 'Of course, sir. I will be throwing all we have at rescuing Miss Gilbert and PC Van Doorn.'

'And the other fellow,' Chief Constable Vickery reminded his subordinate.

'James Butterworth. Yes, sir.'

'What are you doing with that Michaels character?' the chief constable wanted to know. 'The press are going to ask. They love him, you know. He's like some kind of folk hero. Like Robin Hood or something.'

Quinn dropped his gaze to the floor and scrutinised the carpet for a few seconds. Never had Tempest Michaels been more of a problem to him.

'He broke the law, sir.'

'In pursuit of a serial killer, Chief Inspector. The press will have a field day if you charge him.'

Quinn's head snapped up, startled at his boss's attitude. 'You want me to let him get away with it? That would be tantamount to promoting vigilantism, sir.' Was he being tested? The chief constable couldn't want him to set Tempest Michaels and his accomplices free, surely? What possible upside was there?

'Focus on the case, Chief Inspector,' advised the chief constable, his tone fatherly. 'If your team gets a lucky break and finds the Sandman in time, I am sure no one will care what happens to Tempest Michaels. However, as I understand it, your officers have raided a dozen properties currently owned by Ramsey Mitchell and are yet to yield a single clue as to his current location. If the bodies of Karen Gilbert, James Butterworth, and Constable Van Doorn are tomorrow's headline news, who will they blame?'

The subtext hidden in the question hit Quinn like a sucker punch to the gut. Letting Tempest Michaels go was a win-win situation. He could charge them all and release them under caution. Should any of them do anything that sailed even close to breaking the law, he could slam them back into a cell and be guaranteed of a conviction. Better yet though, with Tempest on the outside, he could be certain the man would get straight back onto the hunt. He would even tell Michaels not to, that was bound to make him try twice as hard.

Then, when they inevitably failed to catch the serial killer in time to stop the next round of victims, Quinn could claim the Blue Moon team got in the way, messed with evidence, and ruined his chance of a successful conclusion.

It was genius. Quinn felt like giving a bow to acknowledge his boss's clear thinking. The fact that the chief constable had issued no order on the subject further demonstrated how much Quinn still had to learn.

That was what it took to get to be the chief constable.

Invigorated anew, Chief Inspector Quinn returned to his office ready to do what had to be done. It went against the grain to let Tempest Michaels go now that he had a legitimate reason to see him serve at Her Majesty's pleasure, however, the chance to use the daft paranormal investigator as a tool for his own advancement was too tempting.

Besides, maybe Tempest Michaels would lead him to the Sandman. It wouldn't be the first time the private eye had defied the odds to solve a case.

Cautioned and Released

SATURDAY, DECEMBER 24TH 1206HRS

Tempest

The sleep I knew I ought to grab refused to come for many hours. Processed, stripped of my possessions, and stuffed into a cell in the back of Maidstone station, I was just about angry enough to chew my way out.

The ball of fury in my gut fought for space with the worry I felt for Jane. I'd never believed the Sandman would allow her to live through the night and nothing about that had changed. Held by him and probably unable to do anything about the situation she found herself in, I could do nothing but stew on my failings.

Sleep came eventually, the monotony of incarceration coupled with fatigue forcing my brain to shut down at some point well after midnight.

Quinn never came. His promise to interview us himself either a lie, or an excuse to make sure no one else did it. He would get to me when he was good and ready, that was the message. Had he gone home last night and slept in his own bed while I festered here?

I thought the answer was probably not. He was hard on the case of a serial killer and would want it to be seen that he was throwing himself at it. He would work longer hours and flog himself in a bid to prove his effort in the face of failure. And it would be considered a failure even if he now caught the Sandman because Jane and Jan would be dead.

I figured the time had to be something close to noon. The awful tray of lukewarm breakfast had been served many hours ago, an unpleasant young constable with a dour attitude had posted it through the slot and woke me from my slumber.

I asked him the time and got a stupid response in return.

'Time you bought a watch,' the man's voice had echoed back along the corridor outside.

The tiny slit of hatch opened again now, a set of eyes visible as the officer outside checked to make sure I wasn't poised to attack. To my surprise, the sound of the lock opening then followed.

'Get up,' a man's voice commanded. 'You're being released.'

I shot off the bed. 'Released?'

'Yup. You'll receive a formal caution first. The Chief Inspector wants to see you all.'

He stood to one side so I could leave the cell, his words reverberating in my ears as I slipped around the door. *They were letting us go.*

It made no sense. Quinn wanted to lock me up. He'd been waiting for a decent opportunity for ages. He had one two days ago and could have pursued the charge of firearms possession if he'd chosen to. Two days ago, we had been on better terms, but lying in my cell, I felt sure he would lump that charge in on top of the breaking and entering, wilful destruction of property and whatever else he could cobble together. It might not all stick, but enough of it would that I was looking at a jail sentence.

Now he was letting me go. I felt elated but also troubled by the news.

In the corridor that links the cells, I saw Big Ben being led away too. The officers took us from the cells and back into the police station proper where we were directed toward a row of interview rooms.

A sergeant I didn't recognise was inside waiting for me. He dealt with the official task of reading me my caution and I had to sign to acknowledge that I understood it. With that done, we had to wait for Chief Inspector Quinn to arrive.

I was itching to get out, my legs twitching with impatience to get back to the task of finding the Sandman. Quinn kept me waiting. At least now there was a clock so I could see how much of my life he wasted.

At 1247hrs, he finally waltzed into the room, a breezy smile on his face and a cup of tea in his right hand. He was taking a sip as he closed the door. It made me want to slap the mug across the room. Or maybe see if I could punch it clear through to the other side of his skull.

'Mr Michaels, I appreciate your patience.'

'No, you don't,' I argued. 'What are you up to?' When he shot me an innocent face, I narrowed my eyes at him. 'I know you too well to believe you have the slightest concern about making me wait. Usually, you do it on purpose because you are smallminded and petty and feel some desperate need to score points.'

The Sandman

Basically, I kept throwing insults in his face until the usual version of Ian Quinn returned.

'All right, Mr Michaels, you want to cut through all the nonsense, that's fine by me. I'll tell you why I am letting you go. Right now, I have you on a few charges. I could make them stick and you would probably do some time. It wouldn't be much though, a few weeks perhaps and a lenient judge might take into account your military service and the extenuating circumstances that led you to smash your way into a house. That being the case, you might get community service and walk away from the court laughing.'

I kept my face still. He couldn't make the firearms charges stick. That had to be the case because if he could, he would be throwing the book at me and no judge would let me off so lightly. He didn't have the evidence, just a hunch he couldn't prove.

'I don't like being laughed at, Mr Michaels, so here is what is going to happen. You have already been formally cautioned have you not?'

The sergeant replied on my behalf, 'He has, sir.'

Quinn nodded to himself. 'I am going to release you and because you cannot help yourself, you are going to do something illegal. You always do, Mr Michaels. You have been slipping through my net for months now, but no more. The next time you voluntarily cross the line, I will make sure you go away for a proper spell. Perhaps when you get out, you will have gained some respect for this land's laws.'

A broad grin split my face. Quinn is most likely unaware of it, but he has a tell. When he lies, which he does a lot, he sucks on the left corner of his bottom lip in between sentences or whenever he pauses to think.

He was lying now about his reason for letting me go but

I didn't care. Right now, I didn't care about going to jail either. My mother would have a heart attack and most likely beg God to strike her down rather than face the looks she would imagine at Church on Sunday, but I was going to do what was right without concern for the personal consequences. Was he right that I would break the law? Very possibly. Yet I would do so in a way that would harm no one except those who deserved to be harmed.

'Why are you smiling?' Quinn asked me, his own eyes narrowing. 'Are you going to say something clever, Mr Michaels? I really do not have the will to tolerate any of your rubbish.'

I took a step forward, getting into his personal space. The sergeant scrambled to intervene, but he was the wrong side of the table and couldn't get to us in time.

Not saying anything, I tilted my head to one side, inspecting Quinn's face. When he twitched his eyes in annoyance, I said, 'When you look back months or even years from now, you will wish you had chosen to do the right thing, not the thing that served your immediate ambitions.'

His nostrils flared at my flagrant disrespect for his rank and authority, but he didn't argue, and I think it was because somewhere deep inside he worried I was right.

Ten minutes later, I arrived back in the processing area to collect my belongings. Big Ben, Amanda, and Basic were already there. They were still dressed in their clothes from last night, though they were carrying their Kevlar vests and combat gloves. They all had the dishevelled look of people who had to sleep in their clothes and were offered no opportunity to tidy themselves.

'Everyone doing okay?' I asked. I wanted to offer them a smile, to show the officers around us that we were unbothered by our night in the cells, but I couldn't get my face to comply. While we were locked up what had become of Jane? If there had been a chance to save her before, surely it was long gone now. They appeared to be finished with the process of getting back their belongings; all three were waiting for me.

When the Truth Finally Dawns
SATURDAY, DECEMBER 24TH 1310HRS

Tempest

'What's this?' I asked as the sergeant behind the desk handed back all my possessions one at a time.

He lifted his eyes, looking over the top of his reading glasses to see what I had in my hand. He shrugged. 'It's listed as an electronic device.' Dismissing it, he slid the next item across the counter. 'One G-Shock watch, black.'

He droned on, listing the items as he handed them over. My attention was on the little metallic thing in my hands. It was roughly the size of a thumb drive, but it had no USB connector and no input or output port of any kind that I could find.

I held it up for Amanda to see. 'Any idea what this is?'

She peered at it from across the room. The little electronic gizmo had to have been in one of my pockets though I didn't recall surrendering it when they brought us in last night. Thinking back, I could recall digging my hands into my pockets to then spill everything in them onto the counter. It must have been in with all the other things I carry around.

'Sign here,' demanded the sergeant.

Amanda shook her head. 'It looks like a data storage device,' she observed.

'There's no port,' I pointed out, turning it over and then throwing it across the room to her.

'Hey. Sign here,' the sergeant was becoming insistent.

I swivelled around, gathering the loose change, a handkerchief, and other items from the counter before squiggling my name on the screen to acknowledge receipt.

Amanda and Big Ben were both looking at the gizmo when I got to them.

'It's not yours?' Amanda wanted to know.

'I've never seen it before.' On a different day, with less on my mind, the unexpected presence of a small electronic gizmo might have triggered more questions. Today, I had entirely too many things to focus on, so I took it back when Amanda offered it and slipped it back into my pocket.

I had a bunch of missed calls from my father and several from Jagjit but no messages. I knew I probably ought to call him back to see what he wanted, but heading for the exit from Maidstone police station, it wasn't even going to make it into the top ten on my priority list.

The door delivered us into a walled path that ran along the side of the station and back to the road at the front. It was designed like that to ensure miscreants and lowlifes being released would be kept separate from the decent people coming to the front reception to report a crime in person.

Making our way along the narrow path, Amanda asked, 'What do we do now? Is there a way to pick up the trail again?'

'There has to be,' growled Big Ben, sounding as ready to kill as I felt.

Amanda voiced the problem we all faced. 'But where is he? He wasn't at his house and the police will have uncovered all his other properties by now. If they had caught him, Quinn would have rubbed our noses in it, which means he is somewhere none of us know about.'

I sucked in a breath and started walking. 'We have to go back to the start and work this again. If Jane is st …'

Reaching the pavement at the end of the path, a bright light flared in my face, causing me to jump. Then automatic responses kicked in, driving me off my back foot and forward to attack.

Amanda caught my right arm as it swung backward in readiness to deliver a blow, and in that moment, I saw what was happening.

A microphone appeared under my nose.

'Tempest, tell us what happened last night,' demanded a woman I recognised. 'Are you investigating the Sandman case? What happened in Harrietsham?'

My brain delivered the name I was trying to remember. 'Sarah Gainsworth, yes?' I asked, ignoring all her questions as I recalled the name to go with the face. Then her final question hit me.

Before I could react to it, another microphone appeared, and then another. Cameras were going off, photographers climbing the railings that lined the street to get a shot over the heads of those in front. There had to be thirty or more reporters and journalists lining the street.

'Mr Michaels,' begged a man, 'Are you The Sandman? Is that why they arrested you? Are you guilty of multiple homicides?'

Another voice yelled, 'How many victims are there,

The Sandman

Tempest? Are you going to solve another crime the police are too dumb for?'

Big Ben elbowed his way to the front, smiling for the camera and handing Sarah Gainsworth a card. 'Here you go, babe. Big Ben at your service. The important thing to focus on is how good I look in front of the camera.'

I elbowed him in the ribs and grabbed Sarah's arm. 'You mentioned Harrietsham. What happened in Harrietsham?'

She was taken aback by my aggression, but I wasn't letting her arm go until she talked.

'Two people were attacked in their home and they said a woman was taken. They said there were men wearing robes and they took Karen Gilbert by force after they broke into her house in the middle of the night.'

I felt my consciousness go iffy and started to hyperventilate.

This was me! I led them to her. It had to have been me, and then with that thought came the revelation that I had been dancing to someone else's tune the whole time.

Sensing that my legs were going weak, I ducked my head and sucked in a few breaths.

Amanda came to my aid, gripping both my shoulders and shouting for everyone to get back. She thought I was going to pass out and that made me clench my teeth and fight it.

'How do you know about the Sandman?' I snarled as I came back to upright. The reporters fell silent, keen to hear what I might say next though the cameras continued to click away. Fuelled by the likelihood that I already knew the answer, I shouted, 'Where did you hear that name?'

Shying away from the crazy man who was all but foaming at the mouth, Sarah mumbled, 'It was announced at the press conference. Chief Inspector Quinn told us there is a serial killer in Kent and his team are hot on his tracks. He showed us photographs of the killer's house with a macabre trophy room and said there were dozens of victims to be identified. The chief constable then explained it was Chief Inspector Quinn's team who cracked the case and claimed it was through their diligent work that the Sandman was identified. He never mentioned you but … well, it was leaked that you had been arrested at the scene of the serial killer's house.'

Another reporter, a man, piped up, 'Yeah, this has got spooky written all over it so we figured you must be involved somehow. The police are refusing to comment but the rumour is you blundered in and ruined the whole thing for them. It's your fault the killer got away and was able to claim another victim. Can you comment on that?'

Still reeling from the news about Karen Gilbert, the additional report that I was being cast as the fool spoiling the chief inspector's perfectly crafted raid was the cherry on top.

I wanted to set the record straight. I wanted to explain how Jane was the one who uncovered the Sandman and pieced together the case Quinn was now using. There was no time for that though because I had realised something else.

The Sandman took Jane to lure me in, and he had been one step ahead of me the whole time. He used Jane to involve me so that I would lead them to Karen. I'd been played like a fiddle, but if he was using Jane to make me dance to his tune, there was a very real chance she was still alive.

I grabbed Amanda's hand and swung around to face her while yelling. 'Ben, make a hole!'

The Sandman

As I started to explain my thoughts to Amanda, I got to hear Big Ben chortle, 'Ha, ha! You said, "Hole"!'

The kerfuffle behind me as Big Ben and Basic shoved bodies aside to clear a route for our escape did little to penetrate the hope I now felt.

Amanda grasped it too. It is a dangerous thing – hope. We cling to it when we have nothing else, and risk being hurt all the worse when it proves to be a worthless strategy, yet it was going to drive us forward.

Still holding my hand, Amanda tugged me through the widening gap, speaking over her shoulder as we hurried toward the busy road. 'We need to get back to the office and start again.'

Our cars were in the police station impound zone. We could get them back but it's not exactly a valet service. They would make us wait, and there was no time for any of that.

Big Ben leapt the railing ahead of us, landing in the road where he extended his right hand palm out in a classic 'stop' pose. The driver of a silver Mercedes convertible had to slam on the brakes to stop the car before it hit him.

Behind it, dozens more cars all hit their brakes, the squeal of tyres and the smell of rubber filled the air.

By the time Amanda and I vaulted over the barrier, reporters still throwing questions at our backs and cameras snapping as many shots as they could, Big Ben was dealing with the enraged driver of the Mercedes.

Naturally, the driver just happened to be a sultry-looking redhead twenty-something. Her head was sticking out her window so she could fling insults and profanity at the maniac blocking traffic.

'What the hell are you playing at?' she screamed.

Running across the road, I couldn't help but watch over my shoulder.

'Hello, kitten,' he purred at her, grabbing her roof with both hands, and hanging down so his head filled her window. 'I'm Big Ben, I ...'

The red head shoved the door open, whacking it into Big Ben's chest and shins at the same time. As he reeled backward in shock, she spat some more curses in his direction.

'Big Ben? You ought to be in a mental asylum!' I paused to watch the interplay, gawping with my mouth open because this was something I'd never seen. I mean, Big Ben doesn't score with every woman he meets, but even those who refuse his advances are still wooed by his charming looks and personality.

She stomped on the gas pedal, burning rubber just as he took a step back toward her car and she ran over both his feet.

The cars behind hers all began hitting their horns, wanting to get to wherever they were going.

Visibly trying to ignore the pain in his feet, Big Ben jogged across the road to join us.

Amanda asked, 'Magic wearing off, Ben? Finally, womankind has cottoned on to you? Maybe you shouldn't treat us all like objects.'

'Objects to be cherished,' he defended himself weakly, rubbing his shins. 'I think there might be something wrong with my aftershave.'

Leaving him behind, I started running, a steady pace to get us to the train station where we would find a taxi. We needed new wheels and that meant calling in for reinforcements.

My phone rang, as the traffic picked up behind us, cutting off the reporters though a few of the more determined ones continued to give chase by running to the nearest crossing point.

The word 'Mum' was displayed prominently in the middle of my screen. There had been missed calls from my father already, so with a deep breath, I thumbed the green button to connect the call.

'Mum, what's up?'

'Hello, Tempest. Your father claims that you are not answering your phone. Clearly, he was mistaken or phoning the wrong number perhaps. His brain is getting a little patchy.'

'No, I have a bunch of missed calls from him. I just haven't had a chance to call him back. It's kind of a busy day.' I didn't want to tell her about Jane, and it was going to be a long time (i.e., never) before I let her know I got arrested last night.

'Why, what are you doing?' mum wanted to know.

'Um, it's a bit complicated to explain,' I attempted to misdirect her without actually lying. 'I was planning to not work for the next few days, but something came up. Do you know what dad called for?'

'Something came up?' my mother repeated. 'You mean you're working a case?' she demanded to know. 'It's Christmas, Tempest. You ought to be spending it with family.'

'You are heading to Hampshire, Mother, and we agreed I would spend the time with Amanda and see you in a couple of days.'

'Not if you are working a case, you won't see her,' she argued.

'Amanda is with me, Mother, and this case really will not wait. Is dad there?'

Her voice faded into the distance as she handed her

phone to my father. 'He wants to talk to you,' she muttered grumpily.

'Tempest,' my father's voice boomed in my ear with a jovial edge.

Before he could get into a flow that might be hard to interrupt, I did my best to let him know the call needed to be a short one. 'Hey, Dad. Listen, don't tell mum, but Jane went and got herself kidnapped.'

'Jane?'

'Yes, Dad, Jane, the one I just asked you not to mention to mum. Amanda and I are tracking the person who we think has her, but there is ... well, let's just say I am worried and don't have time to talk, okay?'

'Sure thing, son. I won't take up your time. Go do what you need to do.' That was my dad. He needed enough information to grasp the gravity of the situation, assess it, and make the right decision. Which, in this case, was to aim for brevity and let me get back to what I was doing.

'What did you call for anyway?' I had to ask before I ended the call. He'd been calling me since breakfast according to my phone.

'Oh, err. I'm not sure I should trouble you with it now. It's about the Dickens Museum.'

'Is this about the ghoul?' I asked, latching onto the only recent story about the museum to have reached my ears.

My father repeated, 'A ghoul?'

'Apparently so. I haven't been engaged to investigate it, but there were a bunch of sightings right before the Dickens Greatest Works Theme Park shut its doors a month ago. I know that's not the same place, but I figured the two have a lot in common. Why are you asking?'

Dad took a moment to form a response. 'I spotted something in the paper, a run of coincidences you might say.

One of the shareholders went missing a couple of days ago, some things were stolen from the Dickens Museum, and the shareholder who went missing, well, your mum and I saw him in the bank last week and he was yelling blue murder about not getting a loan he needed. Also, I just met the museum curator, and I'd bet my left nut he's hiding something.'

Honestly, if I hadn't been throwing everything at trying to rescue Jane and catch the Sandman, I would have dropped what I was doing to help him. As it was, I couldn't spare him the time. 'Dad, your best bet is to talk with Frank.' I shot my cuff to check the time. 'He'll still be working, I expect. Try calling him at the shop.'

'I'm standing outside it now,' he let me know.

I needed to finish the call. 'Dad, I've got to go. I'll let you know when I get Jane back. Take care of mum and have a good time in Hampshire.' I knew he would get the information he wanted and hoped that satisfied his curiosity. It wasn't like I needed to worry about him getting involved in trying to catch the ghoul, mum would never allow it.

Scurrying through Maidstone, my brain was whirling with possibilities that the Sandman case could still have an acceptable conclusion. However, there was no hiding the fact that we were a long way from knowing where to find our quarry.

Valerie's Pain

SATURDAY, DECEMBER 24TH 1327HRS

The Sandman

Ramsey Mitchell was having a mixed day. He had Karen Gilbert back and that was cause for celebration. However, the news the police had raided several of his homes came as an unwelcome shock.

It required a change of plans for he would not be able to return to any of his former aliases. Those identities would need to be burned, yet he felt safe where he was. No one knew of his current location and they never would; he'd buried the trail too deep for anyone to follow.

They knew who he was now, he'd seen it on the news, but it didn't matter. He'd been able to perform glorious works, yet he always knew what he needed to do for his Valerie would not be understood. He had failed her, that was the terrible knowledge he could never unburden himself from.

The penalty for that was to suffer every day with the pain of his crime against her. Karen and the others were part of that penance. Valerie's pain demanded it. The women were sent to him, that was what he believed.

Valerie's voice would whisper in his ear, 'Look how much alike she is to me.' She demanded they die, so he would sing them gently to sleep, doing as Valerie insisted, but in a gentle, caring way.

The police were an annoyance, but one he could accept. Ramsey's issue was with Tempest Michaels and the annoying Blue Moon team. Jane Butterworth had no just cause to poke her nose into his business in the first place, and in taking her so he could find his way to Karen, he triggered the rest of them.

That Tempest came to his house last night had been a total shock, but one he played well. Looking back, it filled him with joy to have been so close to being caught only to slip through the hands of his nemesis.

Ha! His nemesis! Ramsey hadn't thought of Tempest Michaels as such before, but it was fitting. Certainly, no one had ever come closer and now he got to demonstrate to his followers and the world just how superior he was by killing the man and his entire team.

They would walk willingly into his trap in their desperate bid to save their friend. All he needed to do was give them a final nudge.

The Blue Moon Office

SATURDAY, DECEMBER 24TH 1336HRS

Tempest

I phoned Jagjit from the taxi, three of us guys crammed in the back because Amanda was swift enough to snag the front seat before the rest of us reacted. So far as we were concerned, that meant she had to pay for the fare plus tip.

'Tempest, where the heck have you been?' Jagjit babbled excitedly. 'No, nevermind, it's not important. You're never going to believe what we found out.'

It turned out that while they did as we insisted last night and went home, they did not crack open the champagne and relax. Following my call from Harry Hengist's house, they got straight back into the research using a copy of Jane's file Alice made at the office.

I gave him a brief breakdown of our evening and how boring it had been, and he understood why he hadn't heard from any of us. Rather than brief me on his discoveries over the phone, he was coming to the office again.

On Christmas Eve, Rochester High Street was as

bustling and busy as it ever gets. Street sellers touted their wares, the smells of mulled wine and frying onions filled the air. We all needed to eat, and boy did I need coffee, so en route to the office on foot because we got the cab to let us out at the far end of the High Street, we split up.

Big Ben went for coffee, probably because he wanted to chat up the girls in there and prove he hadn't lost his touch, and Amanda stopped to snag us some sausages in buns.

Basic came with me to the office. My feet stopped moving the moment I could see the front façade.

There was police tape all over the front door listing the place as a crime scene. Caused to stop walking by the shock of it, I was running the next second. Driven by fury, I tore at the tape, ripping it from the door in a frenzy.

I could see over the frosted panel to the office interior and the mess inside. I was so desperate to get through the door, I almost snapped the key in the lock in my haste.

Throwing the ball of crime scene tape to the floor, I looked around my office. What last night had been a tidy organised space, was now a wreck. The police had come looking for evidence after they arrested us. It was yet another reason why Quinn wanted me locked up last night. With me under arrest, he could legitimately raid my office and take my files.

Now there was nothing we knew about the Sandman case that he didn't also know. The computer tower from the reception desk was missing. Leaving Basic hovering by the door, I ran through the office to confirm they had taken the computers from both my office and Amanda's. Then, getting more incensed with every heartbeat, I ran to the back store. They hadn't just taken the files from the cabinets, the cabinets were gone too.

I heard Amanda swearing and ran back out to find her

just inside the front door. She'd charmed the sausage seller into giving her a cardboard box to carry our food in and was holding it in front of her body as she stared wide-eyed at the desolation of our once-tidy office.

A fresh thought hit my chest like a thunderclap, stopping my heart and restarting it. Yanking out my phone, the battery of which was almost dead after a night in a box at the police station, I called my neighbour.

'Hello, dear,' Mrs Comerforth's answered the phone. 'Will you be home soon? My daughter is coming to take me to her house for Christmas.'

I'd forgotten about that. She told me a few days ago when we were chatting on her doorstep. Being neighbourly, I'd politely enquired as to her plans for the holiday and was pleased to hear she had somewhere to go and people to share it with.

'I'm afraid I will not be home for a while at least, Mrs Comerforth. I'm terribly sorry. When it comes time for you to go, please deposit the dogs back in my house. I will get there as soon as I am able.'

'Very good, dear. I heard your name on the news a little while ago. Did you get arrested again?'

I sighed and hung my head. 'Yes. Yes, I did. I am no longer in custody though. I will be home as soon as I can.' I repeated.

I was still wearing yesterday's clothes, I needed a shower, I was hungry, and we were no closer to catching the Sandman and rescuing Jane than we had ever been. With a heartfelt thank you to Mrs Comerforth and a wish that she would have a happy Christmas, I got off the phone.

Amanda had placed the tray of sausages in buns on the reception desk and was holding her head as she looked around.

'They took everything,' I let her know. 'Even the filing cabinets out back.'

'Hey, folks ... Wow!' Big Ben came through the door with four coffees in a cardboard holder. Like the rest of us, he was shocked at the change from the tidy office we left behind.

'How are we even going to do the research now?' Amanda gasped, pulling at her hair in frustration.

Hampering us probably hadn't been Quinn's primary intention, just a happy side effect. He had all the data, and at some point, he would catch the Sandman.

I took a few breaths to steady myself while I thought.

'Jagjit and Alice are on their way here right now. They have information to share and will have a laptop with them. They also have a car,' Jagjit owns a double cab utility vehicle, 'so if we need to go anywhere, we can.' I was going to need to do something about the dogs and probably wanted to go home to get my own laptop.

Big Ben put the coffees down and grabbed a sausage. Taking a bite, he spoke around the gob of bread and meat in his mouth.

'We have a white board still,' he nodded his head across the room. 'Until Jagjit turns up, why don't we put our heads together and see what we know?'

Big Ben acting as the calm voice of reason was like waking up from a coma to discover ducks had taken over the world and everyone now spoke Belgian. He was right though. Grabbing a bun full of sausage with one hand and a coffee with the other, I went to the board.

We started adding names and notes. The Sandman had three captives that we knew of. He was clearly not at any of the addresses listed under his name because the police would have caught him already. We focused on the probability that he was somewhere not listed against any of his names.

He'd been one step ahead of me since the start, but when we started to talk about that, I had to question what I'd seen when I met him as Harry Hengist.

'I scared him,' I nodded to myself when I said it. The thought had occurred to me before but now I was more certain. 'My arrival at his house was a shock.' I explained my thoughts aloud. 'He could have accused me of attacking him though and be sure I would waste a chunk of my evening keeping the police company.'

'Why didn't he?' asked Amanda, in a tone that acknowledged there had to be a good reason for it.

I thought for a second before concluding, 'Because he believed I would lead him to Karen Gilbert.'

'Which you did,' she agreed, with an apologetic grimace.

I frowned deeply, running the events in Harrietsham through my head. 'No one tailed me there,' I stated confidently.

Big Ben asked, 'How sure are you?'

I puffed out my cheeks and argued with myself. There had been no car following me on the road into the small village. I would have seen it, and there was no one visible in the street when I arrived. They would have needed to be there in advance of my arrival or how could they have seen where I went if they were also not following me. Did the Sandman have a helicopter at his disposal?'

While pondering that question, something the reporters said outside the station came back to me. 'They said there were men in robes,' I murmured, replaying their words in my head.

Amanda said, 'What? Who said what?'

'Men in robes attacked Marion and Buck in their home and dragged Karen Gilbert from it,' I repeated. I doubted that was verbatim what was said but it was close enough.

'Men in robes,' repeated Big Ben, his face taking on a concerned look. 'Basic and me were attacked by a bunch of dickheads in robes when we went to Jane's grans. I told you about that.'

'You never said they were wearing robes,' I argued.

He opened his mouth to argue, but Amanda said, 'It doesn't matter who said what. What does it mean?'

'Do you remember when we left the hospital, I bumped into a chap wearing a black cassock? He was dressed like a monk but clearly wasn't one.'

She got exactly what I was saying. 'This is all connected! They work for the Sandman!'

Big Ben screwed up his face. 'How is that even possible? How can a serial killer have a team of assistants?'

'You said it yourself last night,' I reminded him.

'I did?'

'You said they looked like they were in a cult of some kind. I was too busy to hear what you were saying, or I might have connected the dots sooner.' I was starting to feel sick with all the things I was finally working out. 'I also know how they found Karen Gilbert.'

Everyone watched me fish around in my pockets to find the odd little electronic gizmo.

Holding it up, I mournfully told them, 'I think this is a tracking device.'

Amanda swore.

Big Ben echoed it.

In the silence that followed I doubted I was the only one reeling from the latest revelations. We were not up against one man; we had a force of unknown strength with which to contend. It explained several anomalies such as why the Sandman wasn't wherever Jane and Jan were when I found him at his house last night, and how he managed to snatch three people in a short space of time and overpower Jan in his apartment.

Until this very moment, I had not thought to question how Jan was taken. Big Ben said his apartment was trashed like there had been a fight in it.

The enemy were resourceful, possibly numerous – Big Ben said he fought twelve of them – and had the upper hand in every category. If this were a game of Top Trumps we would lose hopelessly, but it wasn't and now that we knew a little more, maybe we could use it to our advantage.

Big Ben reached out an open hand to me. 'Want to give me that thing? They can try tracking your movements after I turn it into dust.'

I almost gave it to him but snatched it away at the last moment. Holding it aloft, I said, 'This might come in handy yet.'

He jinked an eyebrow at me. 'How so?'

Amanda answered for me. 'They don't know we know. If we can figure out where they are, we might be able to use it to confuse them.'

Sounds coming from the back room of the office drew our eyes as Jagjit and Alice came in.

'Where are your cars?' Jagjit asked. 'The carpark is empty.'

'Still at the police impound yard,' grumbled Big Ben.

Straight down to business, I asked them, 'What have you got for us?'

Dissection of a Serial Killer

SATURDAY, DECEMBER 24TH 1348HRS

Quinn

Chief Inspector Quinn had the attention of a room filled with police officers. That one of their own had been kidnapped got the attention of every police officer instantly, many returning to duty as volunteers despite their shifts ending. They were not just from Maidstone either. The demand to raid more than a dozen properties across Kent drew in teams from constabularies throughout the county, each of them sending a representative to act as liaison.

A tactical team, the same one as earlier, were at his disposal and he was holding court over them all. This was going to be his crowning glory. All they had to do was work the case in a methodical manner, narrowing down the possible locations for the serial killer and his victims until they found them.

Whether the victims were dead or alive would not impact greatly on the magnitude of his achievement, yet he knew he would be conferred hero status if he got to them in time.

Addressing his audience, he clicked the mouse to bring up a new slide.

'This is Valerie Mitchell. Born Valerie Babington, she is presumed to be his first victim. I will hand the floor now to Dr Richard Ventin, a criminal behaviouralist and profiler from Scotland Yard. Dr Ventin.'

Standing back to allow the expert to step up to the microphone, Quinn stopped listening so he could watch to make sure everyone else was. The egghead droned on in a monotone voice, citing various papers on serial killers and their patterns of behaviour. None of it was going to get him any closer to the location of the Sandman but there were a lot of people working on it.

The discovery that Ramsey Mitchell owned and ran a chain of successful locksmith franchises aligned with Jane Butterworth's notes about entering locked properties without leaving anything to indicate someone had. That revelation led almost instantly to one that made his eyes pop out.

Every single one of Ramsey's employees was a criminal. They had all served time in prison, and all had serious psychological issues. Many had committed crimes against women and could most likely be relied upon to do so again given the chance.

That Ramsey Mitchell singled them out for training and employment as his locksmiths explained how it came to be men, not just a man, who broke into the home in Harrietsham to kidnap Karen Gilbert and terrorise the couple living there. That they both survived was amazing.

Dr Ventin was explaining a theory he had about the Sandman trying to recreate an event in his life. In the doctor's words, Ramsey Mitchell was locked into a period when his wife died and that was why he took only women who resembled her.

There was no death record for Valerie Mitchell, but if her husband murdered her, he would not report her missing. She was his first victim, buried somewhere in the Kent countryside no doubt. When they caught him, would they spend years attempting to find the bodies of his victims? Would he have a map somewhere to tell them where each was hidden, or would Ramsey simply not remember?

As a precaution, Chief Inspector Quinn had directed two plain-clothes officers to watch Tempest Michaels and his friends. How they could succeed when he had taken all their information and left them with nothing, he couldn't fathom. He felt sure they couldn't, yet it still felt like a sensible step to keep an eye on them.

Impatient for a call from them, or a breakthrough from the officers trawling through the Blue Moon research, he turned his attention back to the boring profiler.

Locksmiths

SATURDAY, DECEMBER 24TH 1406HRS

Tempest

Jagjit and Alice had been busy, and if the bags under their eyes were anything to go by, they'd had less sleep than us last night.

'It was when you left last night that we started talking about who the real person was,' he explained.

'We had all these different names,' continued Alice. 'But we didn't know which was the real one or if any of them were.'

Jagjit opened his laptop. 'We figured it had to be Ramsey Mitchell because that was the name of the juvenile with the arrest record.'

'That's almost certainly the case,' agreed Amanda.

Jagjit nodded. 'Well, would you believe he's a locksmith?'

Big Ben cursed. 'I knew it!'

It explained the bit where he was getting into properties, but we guessed as much already.

Jagjit got on with telling why that was important before I had to ask.

'He owns a whole firm,' he explained, 'and it looks like all the people he employs are criminals.' He spent the next ten minutes showing us what he meant.

Jagjit used the laptop to show us what he had found and took us to the website for the locksmith business. 'This is it,' he announced.

I stared slack-jawed at the logo. 'Sleep Safe Locksmiths,' I read aloud with a slightly hysterical stutter. 'It's like he's bragging.'

Amanda read the catchphrase beneath the firm's symbol. 'You'll sleep safe with us.'

It was genuinely hard to believe he was so blatant and obvious with it.

Jagjit clicked into the next page which showed vans and smiling locksmiths holding up shiny new keys. Big Ben sputtered out his coffee, making us look his way. He had liquid dripping off his nose.

'That's Smiler,' he jabbed a finger at the screen. Sensing that his comment required more explanation, he said, 'I punched him in the head yesterday. He was one of the fake monks that attacked me in Aylesford. I'd rather like to meet him again, actually.'

I sniffed in a slow deep breath and exhaled again. 'He employs people with a criminal record and uses them to help him commit murder.' It made my stomach turn. 'He killed his wife and has been killing ever since. I'm no profiler but I would be willing to bet this is some kind of weird need to recreate the original act.'

Jagjit said, 'Um.'

We all looked his way. All except Alice who said, 'We couldn't find any record of her death.' When no one said anything, she added, 'There's no obituary for her. We couldn't even find a story about her going missing.'

Amanda scrunched up her face a little. 'There wouldn't be if he murdered her, and no one reported her missing. Given how many houses he has, he could have moved to a new place and no one would have ever noticed his wife was missing.'

Alice and Jagjit exchanged a glance. 'We hadn't thought of that,' Jagjit admitted. 'Actually, we wondered if she might still be alive.'

I shook my head. 'Doubtful.' Moving swiftly on, I said, 'If you found this, the police will already have it, and they will have swooped on his premises hours ago. His assets will be seized, his staff will all be on the run …'

'He's rich,' said Alice.

Amanda hitched an eyebrow. 'How rich?'

Alice had to shrug. 'His father owned a small airline. Ramsey grew up in a mansion. The houses he's bought will be small change to him. He could have millions stashed away somewhere. You said he isn't anywhere the police are looking so we have to assume he's got a place that is off the books. If he has that kind of money, he might be able to move his whole operation to a new place and set up again.'

This was not what I wanted to hear.

'Okay. He's rich, he's got a small army of willing thugs, and we still have no idea where he is. He is here somewhere, and the sun is going down again in an hour. There is no way Jane and the others will survive tonight. That's if they are still alive now. There is something we are missing.'

I wanted to go back to his house and search it again. Of course, the police would have taken everything worth looking at so what I really wanted to do was travel back in time and get a better look yesterday.

A sudden noise jolted me. It wasn't just me; everyone heard it and every head in the office shot around to look at the back door.

Big Ben was already moving, going around us as he started to run. I went with him, but half a second after we heard someone open the back door, we were all running to investigate.

Big Ben got there first, ripping the door open to peer into the barren corridor that led to the carpark.

There was no one there.

Of course, that just prompted us to run to the back door so we could look outside.

Spilling into the carpark, the cold air of late December reminded us that it was necessary to layer up before venturing outside, though none of us were paying attention to the temperature. We were all looking around to spot who might have been at the door.

There was no one in sight. They hadn't thrown in a firebomb, as happened with my last office, and they hadn't left a note.

We hadn't imagined the sound of the door closing though.

Trying to not make it sound like an accusation, I asked Jagjit, 'Did you guys make sure the door was shut when you came in?'

Jagjit looked about guiltily. 'I'm not sure.'

Amanda grabbed my arm. 'There's no one here. It might have been the wind. Let's just get back inside and lock the door.'

We did that, trudging back through to the main part of the office where we were met by a huge surprise.

A Note from the Sandman

SATURDAY, DECEMBER 24TH 1417HRS

Tempest

On the coffee table sat a nondescript cardboard box. It wasn't there when we left, so someone came in the front door as we all ran out the back. Apart from Alice, I think we all saw it at about the same time. The first surprised gasp from her triggered everyone else to look.

I wanted to run at it, worried it might be a bomb or worried for what might be inside and hoping to stop anyone from seeing it. All manner of horrors filled my mind as I made stuttering steps toward it. I both wanted to look inside and wished I would never have to at the same time.

Big Ben barged by me, giving my shoulder a deliberate nudge as he said, 'Pansy.' He made a big act of being braver than everyone else as he strode right up to it when I hesitated, but once poised above it, the nervousness he felt was easy to see.

'Go on, Mr Indestructible,' goaded Amanda, never Big Ben's greatest fan. 'Open it. Just give the rest of us a moment to get behind a wall. We'll all say nice things at your funeral.'

Grimacing because now he had no choice, Big Ben grabbed the box lids, held his breath, and pulled them apart.

Nothing happened.

He'd leaned his head back and turned it away - as if that would make any difference if it were to explode. When it didn't, he opened one eye, swivelled his head around a little and peered at it cautiously.

Since we didn't appear to be about to die, we all crowded around.

Jagjit asked, 'Is it a body part?' The thought made him gag and he had to step away so he wouldn't see when Big Ben reached in to retrieve the box's contents.

'It's a note,' announced Big Ben, pulling a neatly folded piece of writing paper. 'And an old vinyl single.' He snagged it with two fingers. 'Guess what song it is.'

None of us needed to stretch our brains to work out it was *Mr Sandman* by T*he Chordettes*.

Holding the note aloft, Big Ben read it aloud. 'You can have Jane back; I don't want her. If you alert the police, you will never find her or her boyfriend. Then there is a ten-figure reference.'

We crowded around, even Jagjit wanted to see now that he knew there wasn't a head in the box.

Big Ben handed the note over and went to the front door. I watched him, waiting to see if he would spot something, but after a few seconds of scanning outside, he came back inside and locked that door too.

We had been remiss in leaving the doors open, but it had yielded us a result. All our efforts to break this guy down, our hopes to find him before he killed Jane were all for naught because the Sandman wanted to tell us where he was.

'You know this is a trap, right?' asked Amanda in a completely rhetorical way.

I nodded. 'Of course it is. What choice do we have though? If there is even a slim chance we can save any of them, then we have to do it.'

Amanda faced me with a grim expression. 'He's luring us there so he can kill us. The police are all over him. We need to get a tactical unit involved right now.'

Big Ben chipped in, 'She's not wrong, Tempest. If Jagjit is right about this guy having money, then he could be about to pull a vanishing act. If he does that, he can set up some place new and start killing all over again. He wants us, either as punishment for interfering, or because he thinks he is tying up a loose end. Whichever it is, when we go in, we need to have a plan.'

Amanda snorted her disbelief. 'What? When we go in? You just said I was right about needing the police. Armed, trained officers, that's what this situation needs.'

'Babe, I am armed,' said Big Ben, lifting each bicep to his lips in turn so he could kiss them.

Ignoring the giant doofus, I blew out a steadying breath and gathered my thoughts.

'He's been ahead of us the whole time. Everything we have done in the last twenty-four hours is because he did something to make us do it. He had a man waiting for us at the hospital – that's got to be where I picked up the tracker. He had men waiting at Jane's gran's house. He sent someone to deliver this package. If we so much as speak to the police, he will know. I believe we have one shot at getting Jane back and I plan to save her, Jan, and Karen at the same time. I don't know how yet, but it starts with working out where he is and then outthinking him.'

No one said anything for several seconds until I added, 'I'm fine to go alone.'

That created havoc in the office as Amanda started ranting at me and Big Ben got all outraged that I should for one second think he wasn't coming too.

I tapped Jagjit's arm to get his attention. 'I need to see where that grid reference is.'

Hard Choices

SATURDAY, DECEMBER 24TH 1424HRS

Jane

Just like before, I awoke disorientated and alone in the dark with a dry mouth. This time the dry mouth was due to lack of liquid in the last however many hours I had been held captive. Thankful I didn't have a gag to wrestle with, I nevertheless found my ankles and wrists bound again.

A small sob escaped me. It had taken so long to get out of my bindings and then the cell last time, I wasn't sure I had the energy to do it again. My stomach felt like I hadn't eaten in two days, and I wondered if it had actually been that long now. It was long enough that I was becoming weak from lack of food to give me energy.

The fight in the corridor outside came back to me in a flash that had me contort myself around to feel my right leg. The thing I dropped into my boot was still there.

Crunching my aching abs to pull my legs upward, I raised them into the air and wiggled my legs until the thing started moving. It fell from my boot to land on the bed next to me.

Wrestling with two or three or however many of those goons in black robes it was, my right hand came to rest on a pocket. Who knew monk's robes had pockets? I grabbed the object because my brain told me what it was, but there had been no time to do anything with it.

When the Sandman came towards me with a syringe in his hands, it took less than a startled second to comprehend who he was and where I knew him from. It was Karen's neighbour. For the life of me, I could not remember his name, but I remembered tackling him to the carpet believing I had caught her stalker.

That I had been right but let him go stung like vinegar in an open wound.

In that second, when I accepted I was about to go back to sleep, I dropped the thing in my hand down my leg. That it fell into the open top of my boot was blind luck even though it was my aim to do so. Nine times out of ten I would have missed; I'm just not that well-coordinated.

Though my hands were tied together, I could still operate it, thanking my stars that I had something in my arsenal finally as I pushed the catch to release the two-inch blade.

I had a knife. The type that folds into its handle. It wasn't much but it would make short work of my bindings this time.

The lights in the room flashed on, blinding me instantly and burning my eyes through my tightly shut eyelids. Terrified someone was about to come in, I folded the knife under my hands, cutting myself in the process and praying I could keep it hidden.

The door remained resolutely shut, but the speaker boomed into life.

'Ah, Jane, I see you are awake again. You have served your purpose well, my dear, but your usefulness is about to come to an end. I had planned to sing you to sleep myself, but my followers have been not only loyal but deserving of the gift I intend to bestow on them. They will attend to you shortly.'

I tried to fight the ball of terror in my core, but the disembodied voice was so calm and chilling as he talked about ending my life.

'Please make no further attempts at escape. As you will see, your slumber room has been repaired but the plaster is still drying. If you get off the bed, I will have my acolytes beat you. I doubt you will enjoy the experience.'

Overcome by the horror of my situation, I screamed, 'Why don't you just kill me and get it over with?!'

A slow chuckle echoed around my cell. 'Because I need you alive for just a short while longer, my dear. Your friends from the detective agency are coming to try to save you. They are walking into a trap, of course, yet it feels prudent to have you available to halt them, should they achieve more than I believe they can. If you like, I will play their progress over the speaker. That way you can hear them die one by one.'

I was hyperventilating. Lying still on the bed, I couldn't seem to get any oxygen into my lungs. I always knew Tempest and the others would be doing all they could to find me, but now I wished they weren't.

Were they really walking into a trap? I'd seen Tempest achieve the unbelievable more than a few times. And his friend, Big Ben, well he might be little more than a walking penis, but he was a fighting machine. The pair of them were trained soldiers with a shadowy past. Would they really be suckered in and killed so easily?

If the Sandman's confidence were any marker, they didn't stand a chance against him and they were just two against a cohort of his robed helpers. He called them acolytes. It made it sound as if this were a cult or a religion.

The knife was still tucked under my hands, but any thoughts I had about using it to free myself had to go on hold for I held no doubt about his willingness to punish me if I tried to get free. A chance would come. The question was whether I would be able to use it to free myself, or if the option I would take would be to kill the Sandman.

Though it terrified me to even think it, I knew the only way to stop him, might be to sacrifice myself.

Hidden Things

SATURDAY, DECEMBER 24TH 1428HRS

Tempest

'Does this look right?' asked Jagjit.

I turned my head to look at his screen. He'd navigated to an Ordnance Survey map where the ten-figure grid reference could be translated into a position on the planet.

When I saw where it was, I did a double take.

'I know this place!' I blurted.

Amanda swivelled around to look at what had me excited and the others crowded around to see the screen.

Basic was still finishing off the now cold sausages in buns. Most of us had eaten a couple, all except Alice and Jagjit who had been at home all day and able to eat when they wanted to. Basic was on his fifth or sixth and I hoped they gave him energy because we were going to need it.

My claim to know the place we were looking at was doubly true. It was inside a country park where I occasionally walked my dogs, but I also saw it just a few hours ago. It was on a map on the desk inside Harry Hengist's house. At the time, I spent a few seconds looking it over and wondering about its significance. I hadn't recognised it though. Not at the time. Now I did.

'That's Cobham Country Park,' said Alice, recognising it too.

'Oh. So it is,' agreed Big Ben.

With a finger, Alice traced the A2 dual carriageway as it passed the location on the map. A main artery bisecting Kent, it led directly from Dover to London. Anyone familiar with the county could recognise the towns and villages on the map before us.

I told them about the map in Harry Hengist's house. 'There's something you probably don't know about that park,' I told them all.

Amanda asked, 'What about it?'

I pointed to a small mark on the screen and had Jagjit zoom in. It appeared as a series of dashes that made a line. It indicated something buried beneath the ground. I only knew what it was because I had been there and stumbled across it once.

'There is a second world war operations room beneath the ground.'

Jagjit's jaw dropped open. 'You have got to be kidding me.'

'There's nothing labelled on the map?' questioned Alice.

I nodded. 'That's because secret stuff doesn't get labelled. It's there. There is a plaque erected to tell people what it is, but it is sealed up. At least, it has been whenever I have passed it. I walk the dogs there sometimes,' I explained. 'The only indication on the surface is a barrier to stop people falling into the hole where the stairs go down to a door. The surface is completely flush with trees and stuff growing on top.'

'How many ways in are there?' asked Big Ben, his business face was showing, and he was thinking tactically.

Six sets of eyes scoured the map.

'There.' Amanda jabbed a finger at the screen. We spent minutes looking for another set of dashed lines but could find none. There were two ways in. Both would be locked under normal circumstances, yet if the Sandman were using it as a lair and wanted to lure us in, I figured at least one door would be open. The grid reference took us to one of the doors, not the other.

Big Ben growled, 'We need to tool up. Did the cops leave anything in the back?'

He referred to our chest of weapons, some of which we'd taken to Harry's house yesterday. I'd already checked though, and the whole thing had been taken at the same time as the filing cabinets. No doubt Quinn had his forensics chaps testing them to see if he could match blood to a crime.

'Okay,' I said as forcefully as I could muster – mostly for my own benefit. 'It's time to go.'

Amanda sounded shocked when she said, 'Wait, what? We need to have some kind of plan first, surely. You already said this was a trap.'

I paused to tighten the Velcro on my Kevlar stab vest. 'I have a plan. I'll explain it on the way.'

'What about weapons?' asked Big Ben.

'We'll get those on the way too.'

Outside the office, the streets were filled with people excited for Christmas. Midnight was only hours away and the sun was on its way down.

While the world around us revelled in the joys of the holiday season, we were going to storm a madman's underground fortress, take on a force of unknown size and attempt to rescue three people. It was foolhardy beyond belief, and I felt no choice but to do it anyway.

I had just one ace up my sleeve and it was based entirely on a hunch. The Sandman was too confident. He believed we were going to do exactly as he demanded, and he was right, sort of.

The bunker in Cobham Woods was a trap. A dead end where he could easily trap us, but an underground bunker with just two access points was a trap for those already inside too. Something about it did not feel right, by which I mean, I didn't believe he was going to allow us to corner him there.

Leaving the back of the office to pile into Jagjit's car, I fingered the tracking device in my pocket and failed to notice a shadow lean out from the wall opposite.

Reason to get Excited?

SATURDAY, DECEMBER 24TH 1441HRS

Quinn

'Copeland what have you to report?' Chief Inspector Quinn had been anxiously waiting to hear from his plain-clothes men. With fifty officers in a hastily requisitioned school gymnasium, the task of sifting through all they had taken from the houses owned by Ramsey Mitchell and from the Blue Moon office was going well, but it was yet to yield a result.

There was just too much data. From the house in New Ash Green alone there was enough paperwork, documents, books, photographs, and other items to keep a team going for a year.

Yet the clock was ticking, and it grew dark outside. He couldn't tell how much of James Butterworth's research could be trusted, and it was clear from the odd crossdresser's notes that he was guessing most of his conclusions about the serial killer. However, his belief that the victims would be killed the night they were kidnapped was not only plausible but likely.

It meant James Butterworth and Constable Van Doorn were already dead. It was annoying but if that were the case, there was nothing he could do about it. Saving Karen Gilbert would be enough to ensure he was recognised. There would be a commendation at least.

Constable Bob Copeland peeled out of the shadow behind the Blue Moon office in Rochester as he watched the utility vehicle gather speed over the cobbled road.

'They are moving, sir,' he gasped into his radio as he ran.

He'd been given warning they were heading his way by his partner for the night, Constable Danny Hurst. Danny was watching the front which at least gave him something to look at. Standing in the shadows behind the office was boring. Bob was cold and his feet had gone to sleep an hour ago.

Neither man complained though. They both knew Jan and knew the code: we do everything to protect our own.

Danny was already at the car, clambering into the driver's seat when Bob arrived.

'They are in a car, sir,' PC Copeland reported. 'We are following.'

'Good,' murmured Chief Inspector Quinn. 'Stay with them. Let me know where they go.'

'There's something else, sir,' Bob added. 'Two men came to the office about half an hour ago.'

Quinn found he was squinting, desperate to hear what the man might say next.

'Sir, one opened and shut the back door to get their attention, and the other ducked inside to leave a box in their office. Both then ran away. We didn't see where they went, but they were wearing black robes, sir.'

Bob didn't say it but had been worried about revealing this little snippet of information. The chief inspector was a harsh critic and unforgiving if anyone did anything he thought was the wrong thing to do. He discussed what they ought to do with Danny at the time but both agreed their orders were to watch the Blue Moon team so that was what they did.

Quinn's heart beat a quick staccato. This could be exactly what he was hoping for.

'Stay on them, keep me informed and whatever you do, do not let them out of your sight. If you lose them, don't bother coming back unless it's to clear out your lockers. Out.'

With the call ended, the two constables shared a worried look. They were following the Blue Moon team but had to try to look like they were not following. There was no back up team that could swing into position if the people ahead spotted their tail. Cautiously, and trying to keep at least one car between them, they drifted along in the wake of the utility vehicle.

Tooling Up

SATURDAY, DECEMBER 24TH 1520HRS

Big Ben

Jagjit's car could easily seat five, but there were six of us which made it a squeeze. I offered to have Alice sit on my lap in the back. I was just trying to be helpful, but Jagjit eyed me as if I might be trying to achieve some other aim.

I guess I understood his concern. More than a few seconds breathing in my heady scent while pressed against my muscular form was bound to make his wife reconsider her poor choice of partner.

So I got to ride in the front where my broad frame and long legs had room to fit. I pulled my chair forward a bit to give those behind as much room as possible, but it was still cozy back there with four of them stuffed in.

Following Tempest's instructions, we went over the bridge into Strood and through the small town, stopping at a hardware store on the way out. It was due to shut until Boxing Day in less than an hour but that was more time than we needed.

Tempest and I both grabbed trolleys, a small procession of us heading through the electronic double doors when they swished open.

We got looks from everyone who saw us. I'm used to it, of course, because there is barely a woman on the planet who doesn't stop to get at least a second glance. The men were looking too though, and it was entirely because four of us were wearing our black combat gear again.

The fingerless gloves with the Kevlar knuckles had a purpose, but in such a benign, civilian setting, we looked like a paramilitary team.

Naturally, anyone looking would assume I was the leader.

Spotting an attractive member of staff in her thirties, I sashayed up to her. 'Hey, babe, I'm Big Ben. Can you point me toward the chainsaws, please?'

When she looked my way, I hit her with the smile that had dropped a thousand knickers.

Something went wrong with it because she raised an eyebrow and jerked a thumb toward the back of the shop.

'Aisle twelve.'

Amanda hooked my elbow. 'Come on, Romeo. We don't have time for anything else.'

Starting to panic because my batting average in the last twenty-four hours was zero hits from a lot of swings, I found myself mumbling. 'I need to find a mirror.'

'No time,' Amanda repeated.

'But there's something wrong and I worry that if we don't fix it the world will stop spinning.'

I heard her say something like, 'Dear Lord,' as she let go my arm and jogged to catch up with Tempest.

What was happening to me?

Doing my best to put it from my mind, I found the

chainsaws and loaded two into the trolley along with a can to carry the fuel I would need.

Tempest and the others were all heading for the tills by the time I found them, their trolley near overflowing with tools that made very good weapons yet were completely legal to buy and carry in public. It was using them as a weapon where the line got crossed, but we were so far past the point of caring about that now I doubted it even surfaced in anyone's mind.

Updated Information

SATURDAY, DECEMBER 24TH 1603HRS

Quinn

'Where are they now?' Quinn snapped out his question when Copeland's voice came through it again.

'At Big Jobs hardware store in Strood, sir. They are buying tools. It looks like they are planning to renovate a house, sir.'

Quinn rolled his eyes. 'They are tooling up for a fight, you idiot. Did you see what they bought?'

Copeland's eye flared. What kind of people was he dealing with here? He knew of Tempest Michaels; everyone did. The TV footage of him making Quinn look like an idiot was saved to the phone memory of every officer in Maidstone. It had happened more than once too.

Copeland heard the stories about them just the same as everyone else and had been in the grounds of Rochester castle in October when a huge battle broke out between two gangs of clowns. The whole thing was utterly bizarre, but surely the other tales were all hyperbole?

Whether they were or not, he had to now question what the Blue Moon investigators thought they were going up against with chainsaws, battery-powered nail guns and sledgehammers. Yet more items were loaded into the back of the utility truck's load bed, most of them in boxes so he couldn't make out what they might be.

Eyeballs poking out on stalks, he saw the Indian guy and the woman who wasn't Amanda Harper head back to the store. He recognised Amanda because she only left the police a few weeks ago. Bob didn't know what they were going back for, but the moment they were far enough away, the big guy jumped into the driver's seat and a second later the car rocketed out of the carpark.

The Indian guy and the woman were left staring at the receding taillights looking speechless, but Bob only caught a glimpse of them as Danny stomped on the accelerator to give chase again.

A Plan

SATURDAY, DECEMBER 24TH 1605HRS

Tempest

From the backseat, Amanda said, 'You didn't have to do that, you know.' She was less than impressed with me.

I sucked some air in between my teeth, unhappy that I had done it too.

'I couldn't risk Jagjit refusing to hand over the keys or trying to come with us.' I wasn't happy that Amanda was coming with me either for that matter. It wasn't a question of her ability to manage in a crisis situation; far from it. I was in love with her and putting her in harm's way as I was about to did not sit well.

'He would have understood,' she argued.

'There was no time to discuss it,' I insisted. 'Jagjit is too proud to have accepted me leaving him behind without arguing to save face. His wife was there to witness it, so he would have felt it necessary to fight me on the subject. We don't have time for that.'

Amanda either conceded the point or she chose to save

her breath. Either way, she had nothing more to say and the car lapsed into silence interspersed only by the sound of Basic's *Gameboy* playing music as he fought to save *Princess Peach*.

From Strood to Cobham is a straight shot through the centre of town and up the A2. It was also known as Watling Street and followed the line of the original road built by the Romans to connect Dover (Dubris) to London (Londinium). It took ten minutes to get to the exit, leaving the busy road and the traffic heading to the capital as we swept down the off ramp and into the dark countryside.

At this time of year, mere days after the winter solstice, the sun literally fell from the sky when it decided the day was over. An hour ago, it had been light. Now it was full dark.

Would that play into our hands or not?

Big Ben killed the lights with a mile to go to the park, and dumped Jagjit's car at the side of the road when he found a lay by it would fit in. We were still four hundred yards shy of the park entrance, but the gate would be shut by now to stop people going in there at night and we needed to be invisible as we approached.

Using boot polish bought at the hardware store, we buddied up to black out each other's faces, removing any shine that might catch the moonlight to give our position away. After a quick check to make sure we could move silently without things in our pockets jangling, we hefted the tools from the load bed, loading as many as we could into pockets and belts and carrying more besides.

We overdid it at the store, buying more than we could comfortably carry, but that was okay – we had enough.

And we had a plan.

Remember the keys?

Preparation is Everything

SATURDAY, DECEMBER 24TH 1618HRS

The Sandman

Ramsey Mitchell finished shaving and dabbed his face and neck dry with a towel before applying some moisturiser and a touch of aftershave. He needed to feel the part and for that he knew he also needed to look the part. As if he were going out on an important date, he was taking the time to make sure he looked and smelled good.

Karen was a special one for several reasons. Partly it was because she had slipped through his fingers and he'd thought her lost. Regaining her brought him such joy. The other reason was because of how closely she resembled his precious Valerie.

If it were true that a person had a type, then Valerie was his. That was how, as a young man, he came to hurt her. It had never been his intention to do so, but she had been making him pay for his error ever since. Her constant instructions gave him purpose and only by obeying them could he please her.

Returning to his control room, with the screens and the radio, he checked the position for Tempest Michaels. He had considered phoning him to draw him out but doing so left him exposed to being questioned by the man and he knew the police were looking for him already.

He doubted they would be able to find him, but prudence demanded he wrap things up here and move on. Besides, sending the note was more elegant in many ways and had proven to be just as effective.

The little blip on his screen didn't tell him if anyone else were with Tempest, but he felt secure in his belief that the giant would be with him, and the dumb one who looked like a caveman. Probably the pretty blonde one too. He'd read of their exploits and had a mental picture for how they operated. They were a frontal assault, blunt force instrument.

They would sense the trap they were walking into and choose to rely on luck and courage to see them through. They would not last long.

The wall to his front contained six monitors, each of which could display the feed from one of many cameras. Only one had a picture currently because the others were all in darkness. He flicked switches on the console, bathing both the police officer, Constable Van Doorn, and Karen in bright white light.

Both were awake and had to shield their eyes.

Clearing his throat, and licking his lips, the Sandman leaned toward his microphone and switched it to address all areas so not only would his acolytes hear it, so would the three forms in their slumber rooms.

'Good evening one and all. Most especially you, Karen, my precious. Tonight is to be a celebration. You have been chosen. Chosen to be saved. Before we get to the ceremony,

I wish to allow you to listen to the foolhardy attempt to rescue you from the sanctuary I offer. Tempest Michaels and his friends are about to storm my bunker. I would like you all to listen as they die.'

Full Assault Mode

SATURDAY, DECEMBER 24TH 1623HRS

Big Ben

As Tempest predicted, the bunker door at the front was unlocked. This was the scariest part of what we were going to do, but Tempest's plan was either genius or suicide; we would find out which soon enough.

With Basic at my side, I edged into the darkness. Some night vision goggles would have gone down well, right about now, but the moment I thought that the lights came on.

Blinking against the sudden light and sticking to the walls to minimise the target we might offer them, I gritted my teeth and took in my surroundings.

We were in a tunnel made from concrete. It went about eight feet before it met another staircase that went down again. I peered cautiously over the edge. The stairs went down maybe fifty yards into the earth. It would have been well protected from the bombs the Germans dropped all over the county during the second world war. Whoever had been working down here would have been safe.

I didn't bother to turn to look behind me, I simply took the jerry can of fuel I had prepared, lit the rag, and threw it. As it sailed through the air, I started down after it. Not too fast, I didn't want to be too close when it hit the floor below and exploded.

With a boom that was like a concussion grenade going off, the plastic jerrycan hit the ground far below and a fireball filled the air. I heard screams of terror and some of pain and the shock that goes with it but had to hunker down and hug the stairs as a burning ball of flame shot back up at me.

I intended to cause shock and awe, and to capitalise on that I had to move now and move fast. Basic was right on my heels, a sledgehammer in each hand as we both ran down the concrete steps as fast as we could. A sled would have worked better but might have been going too fast to control once we hit the unforgiving floor below.

Screaming like a banshee I came into the bottom tunnel to find fake monks in their daft dresses running away. Some were half undressed, the robes discarded having caught fire. There was nothing in the tunnel to burn but the smell of charred cloth and hair hung in the air.

We were in.

All the Fuel I Would Need

SATURDAY, DECEMBER 24TH 1627HRS

Jane

To say I felt sick wouldn't even come close. When the Sandman stopped speaking, there was silence for more than a minute before the sound of an explosion made me think Tempest had borrowed a tank from somewhere.

Honestly, I wouldn't put it past him.

The ripping noise of a chainsaw filled the air. There were shouts, Big Ben's voice easy to pick out, so too Basic's.

There were shouts from people I didn't recognise – the Sandman's acolytes no doubt.

I had no idea how many they had to face or how far they had to go to get to me. How vast was the building I was in?

'Get them,' growled a voice I didn't know. The malice in it did nothing to belie the owner's intentions. They were sent there to kill and sounded joyful at the prospect.

'Now!' shouted Tempest. 'Go now!' His voice was easy to pick out from the other cries filling the air. However, his shout was followed by a cry of pain and my breath caught in my throat.

I could only hear them over the speaker. They were trying to get to me, but they had to be on another floor high above me, or at least so far away that the sounds of their struggle couldn't reach me through the walls.

'Tempest is down,' shrieked Amanda, trying to stay calm but failing.

A sob escaped me.

'Where are they?' yelled one of the acolytes.

An answer came back. 'I can't see! There's too much smoke.'

A grunt of pain followed by a blood-curdling wail from Basic made me curl into a ball on the bed. My friends were all dying in their bid to save me. If I could have been more vigilant, I would have seen the Sandman coming for me. I should have been watching. Or I should have tried harder to work out who he was. If I had solved the case already, none of this would be happening.

'Where's Tempest?' shouted Big Ben. 'We need to retreat!'

Amanda's words ripped right through my heart. 'He's dead, Ben. We're cut off!'

Big Ben's enraged war cry filled the airwaves and was abruptly silenced.

Only the sound of Amanda's terrified crying remained.

'I think that will do,' said the Sandman, cutting the feed so I didn't have to listen to them find Amanda.

I still had the knife and I had a belly filled with lava that was ready to erupt. I might only get one chance to kill him, but if the opportunity came, he had given me all the fuel I would ever need to gladly exchange my life for his.

For what he had done, he needed to die.

Behind Every Great Man

SATURDAY, DECEMBER 24TH 1638HRS

Jane

They came for me less than a minute later. I sat up on the bed as the door opened, keeping the knife tucked inside my hands so it couldn't be seen. It didn't take much effort to look terrified and defeated – I was both.

The first man had horrible teeth. He smiled at me, showing off how many were broken, missing or crooked.

'Evening, gorgeous,' he slurred, sounding a little drunk. From his sleeve he pulled a knife. Not a little thing like the one I had tucked out of sight, but a footlong blade that could gut me in a second.

Involuntarily, I sucked in a petrified breath, but he sunk to his knees to cut through the bonds around my ankles.

'Try kicking anyone and I'll kill you slowly,' he promised, rasping into my face with breath that stank of cheap whisky.

He backed away, two other men coming around him to grab my arms and lead me from the cell.

Walking toward what I felt certain was the end of my life, I knew I expected my legs to feel weak or just refuse to work. Somehow though, having accepted I was going to die shortly, I felt something akin to serenity. My only hope was for the chance to kill the man behind it all. I couldn't save Jan, who was being bundled along the corridor ahead of me, thrashing and struggling against his captors. Or Karen, who I could hear begging and whimpering as she was hauled from her cell.

The acolytes holding Jan paused to administer a few punches, hard blows to his gut and kidneys that persuaded him to stop fighting for a few moments.

At the end of the corridor, farther than I had gotten in my failed escape attempt, I was greeted by the sight of the Sandman himself.

His arms were aloft, framing his face and the broad smile it bore.

'Acolytes, your brothers have fought bravely against the fools who stood against us. Tempest Michaels and his friends are no more. They tried to damage our mission, and though they have inflicted wounds, they gave their lives to do so. We will rejoice now and when the ceremony is complete, we will move on. I have a new place for us to call home, and you will all be welcome there. Our mission must continue. Bring forth those who we honour tonight. Your victorious brothers will be waiting outside to join with us.'

He turned around and began to lead the procession. Around a corner we reached a set of wooden stairs leading upward. They were poorly lit and narrow, the men either side of me having to switch so only one had me in his grasp. It gave me a chance to adjust my grip on the knife.

I was ready, but I had ten people between me and the Sandman.

At the top of the stairs, I was surprised to find myself inside a house. It was dimly lit and sparsely decorated, but a house, nonetheless. The creak of floorboards beneath my feet gave an indication of its age.

We were heading for the front door; I could make it out between the heads of those in front of me. I thought we were going to go straight out but the procession halted at a door to a room on the left.

'Are you ready, my love?' asked the Sandman.

I found myself frowning. Who was he talking to?

When a woman emerged from the room a second later, a choked gasp escaped my mouth and closer to her, Karen screamed in fright.

Hyperventilating again, my eyes refused to believe what I was looking at. Framed by the light above her head, which cast ugly shadows onto her face, the woman was ghastly to look at. Her face would haunt anyone who ever saw it.

Her right eye was an empty socket, and a good portion of the hair on that side of her head was missing, giving way to terrible scar tissue beneath. She looked to have melted. Unable to take my eyes off her, I observed the fallen cheekbone and the hole in her cheek through which I caught a flash of a white tooth when she moved her jaw.

A hand flashed out, slapping Karen across the right side of her face. It silenced the poor, terrified woman but only for a heartbeat as the same hand then grabbed hold of her hair, twisting it cruelly.

'This is your fault!' the deformed woman rasped. 'You did this to me. That is why you must pay.'

'What?' whimpered Karen. 'What did I do? I don't know who you are?'

'I was beautiful once,' the woman raged. 'But a slut like you caught my husband's eye.'

Oh, my God! She's the Sandman's wife!

'He cheated on me,' the woman sneered with a grimace at her husband. The Sandman hung his head in shame. 'Didn't you? You worthless maggot. So I tried to take my own life. Do you know what happens when you pour acid over your own face?'

Karen looked like she might vomit. There was no colour in her face and if she was expected to answer, I doubted she were able.

The hideously disfigured woman continued talking, providing an answer to her own question. 'You have to spend the rest of your life in hiding, but your husband does anything you ever tell him to. Including finding other pretty young sluts to pay the price for his indiscretion.' Her voice was an ugly snarl that sounded right at home coming from her face.

'But I didn't do anything,' Karen snivelled, her voice cracking to become a hoarse whisper.

The Sandman's wife snorted a laugh. 'And soon you never will. Isn't that better than ruining a marriage?'

As if on cue, an acolyte at the front door pulled it open and stepped outside.

The woman turned to go and as she did I saw the other side of her face. It was unblemished, and she was beautiful. In her sixties, but attractive nonetheless, the standout detail was how much she looked like Karen.

The wave of understanding hit me so hard it felt like I had been plunged into a vacuum. It wasn't the Sandman choosing the women he killed. He wasn't the one driven to murder them, it was his wife!

My brain was reeling, trying to add things up and it was then that I realised what was amiss. I heard explosions and

The Sandman

shouts about fire when Tempest and the others stormed the building yet there was no smell of smoke.

If the Sandman's acolytes defended the building and overwhelmed my friends, why were they going to be waiting outside like the Sandman just said?

Unable to conjure answers, I became even more confused when I arrived outside because there were no acolytes waiting there.

Looking impatient, the Sandman checked his watch and lifted a radio to his mouth.

'Bunker team, where are you? We are starting the ceremony with or without you.'

The radio crackled. 'Oh, don't do that,' begged Tempest.

How it Went Down

SATURDAY, DECEMBER 24TH 1630HRS

Big Ben

Tempest's plan was about as mad as any he has ever concocted. We were going to storm the bunker, fake our own deaths and in the ensuing confusion caused by smoke and fire, we would overwhelm them.

In the hardware store, we bought the best breathing masks they had; ones that would filter out smoke. We also bought fire retardant spray with which we doused our clothes, and airtight goggles to protect our eyes.

When Basic found a t-shirt gun on a promotional end, we bought three of them and all the t-shirts they had. They all got doused in petrol.

While Basic and I went in the front, shouting instructions to Tempest and Amanda as if they were with us, Tempest was going in through the other door. He took bolt croppers and an oxyacetylene torch just in case, but the key on the big ring he took from the Sandman's house in New Ash Green opened the lock.

The police had it in their possession but gave it back to Tempest when they released him. Whoever was inside expected us to come from one direction, and we were bang on that coming at them from both ends would throw them completely.

With a wall of fire before us, we drove them back far enough to get inside. We didn't need to look for flammable material because the t-shirts provided it. They worked better than I could have predicted but we had to pretend to die before the smoke caused the dress-wearing nutbags to flee.

It was a difficult balance: they had to be blinded to our movements, but not so much they would know we were acting. Divided to fight on two fronts, each thought the other was winning. The reports of our deaths fuelled their confidence and as smoke filled the bunker and they needed to escape it, they came forward. Spread thin, coughing and choking from the smoke, we picked them off like apples on a tree.

If you are wondering why we weren't worried about setting fire to the whole place or of accidentally killing Jane and the others, the answer is Tempest guessed.

On the way to the hardware store, he told us about the map he'd seen at Harry Hengist's house. Cobham Woods and the old bunker was marked on it, but so too was a second building. There was a small annotation on the map, made in pencil. Tempest could not recall what it said but believed that was where the Sandman would be.

Not in the bunker.

His guess was based entirely on a single premise: the Sandman wanted us to go to the bunker and expected us to die there. If that was where he wanted us, it would not be where he was. He would have to be close by though and the only structure for more than a mile in any direction was this odd little house in the middle of nowhere.

Genuinely, I found it a little annoying that he was right.

Each of the dickhead monks got cable tied around their wrists and ankles with their hands behind their backs. A third cable tie connected the first two together – they were going nowhere. The joy of coming in from both sides was that we could be certain none of them had been able to get out and a trap intended for us worked against them.

The Sandman might be top drawer material when it came to being a psycho serial killer, but he was rubbish at military strategy.

Once sure we had them all, Tempest jogged back to his end to open the door and the through draft swept the smoke out. It had been slick and swift but the part of the job we had done wasn't the part we needed to do, it just teed us up nicely for it.

Knowing I only had a few seconds before we needed to get moving, I checked the hogtied dickhead monks looking for one man in particular.

Grabbing one by the hair to turn his face my way, I asked, 'Where's Smiler?'

He didn't respond and I realised he was unconscious.

I moved to the next one, 'Where's ... ah, nuts.' He was out cold too. 'Are any of you idiots still conscious?'

I got no answer, but someone coughed.

'A-ha! Where are you?' Quiet ruled. For a second anyway. Then he couldn't hold the cough inside any longer and that showed me where he was. 'Where's Smiler?' I demanded, getting in his face.

He was trying hard to squirm away but tied up as he was, there was no way to escape me.

'Who?' he blurted, still wriggling to get free.

'Calm down. I won't hurt you if you just answer my question. I'm Big Ben, what's your name?' I asked, giving the man a reassuring smile.

I got a mad look back as he tried to reflect my smile. 'Carl. I'm Carl. I'm really new here. I'm not really with these guys. I just …'

'Yeah, yeah, yeah. I don't like Carl as a name. I think I'll call you Susan. So come on, Susan. Where's Smiler? You know. He's got a gob full of broken teeth.' It was a good enough description so far as I was concerned.

Stuttering, the man said, 'That's Marco. He's one of the master's favourites. He is with him.'

Tempest loomed over me. 'At the house?' he asked the dickhead monk.

I prodded him. 'Answer please, Susan.'

The man nodded vigorously. 'That's right. They are all at the house getting ready for the ceremony. Marco is being given the girl.'

'Karen?' Tempest tried to clarify.

This time Susan shook his head. 'The blonde one.'

I stood up. It was time to go. There was rescuing to do. Tempest was already leaving, indicating to Amanda and Basic to go because we were coming.

I took a step, then stopped myself. 'Whoops. Almost forgot.'

I know it's wrong to hit a man when he's down, but I don't think that rule really applies to evil cult members who murder people for fun.

Susan went night night for a while.

Ambush My Ambush

SATURDAY, DECEMBER 24TH 1638HRS

Tempest

Four of us had taken out five times that number in less than two minutes. If we lived through this, I was going to record it as a massive victory and mark it on my calendar as a day to celebrate. We still had the biggest part of this to do though.

We had to confront the Sandman and however many men he had left – it could be one, ten, or a hundred – and he had three hostages to use against us.

This was far from over.

Finding the house was easier than I expected – we could see it only moments after leaving the bunker behind. It was a manmade structure poking up through the trees less than a mile away. It took us under eight minutes to get there and would have been less if Basic could run faster.

I wasn't going to complain, I had no right to say anything negative to a man who volunteered to put his life on the line.

The Sandman

We all had two radios now. Our own ones, and another one each taken from the monks in the bunker. It enabled us to listen in to their radio net though we dared not employ them yet. Just as we arrived at the front of the little house, the front door opened.

I watched them leaving the building, filing out in a long line. There were maybe a dozen idiots in their black monk's robes, plus the man I met as Harry Hengist. He had a woman on his arm, and the sight of her face sent a shocking chill through me because I recognised her even with the terrible scars.

She'd aged since someone took the picture I'd seen in Harry's bedroom, but then several decades had passed. However, there was no mistaking that I was looking at Valerie Mitchell, the Sandman's wife. I was rooted to the spot for a beat while my brain worked the new information.

She wasn't shackled in any way, and she did not look scared or upset unlike the three captives being hauled along by the Sandman's acolytes.

Before I could consider it any further, the Sandman lifted his radio and spoke.

'Bunker team, where are you? We are starting the ceremony with or without you.'

I pressed the button and felt a smile crease my mouth for the first time in days. 'Oh, don't do that.'

Big Ben took that as his cue and started running.

A supressed pfft, pfft, pfft noise was just about audible as Amanda, hidden from sight somewhere to my right began firing nails at the crowd. Gathered together as they were, they made an easy target and she scored multiple hits in the first seconds.

I was running too, closing the distance because this was a close quarter fight. The way to stop them using Jane, Jan, and Karen as hostages was to get them back before anyone knew what was happening.

Our strategy was to get the captives back. Nothing else mattered. That said, if I got a chance to kill the Sandman, I was probably going to do it and I doubted Big Ben was going to shake any hands.

The four of us had spread out so we came at them from multiple directions, all screaming like berserkers as we crossed the open ground. We were exposed once we left the shadow of the trees, but our attack came so fast and was so unexpected that we caught them completely unprepared.

I heard a roar on my left as Basic met the first of the Sandman's men and saw the edge of a sledgehammer catch the light as it scythed over his head.

Half a second later it hit someone in the chest. That person went down like a cannonball had hit them and they did not get up.

Each of us had a specific target – one of the captives. Basic was getting Karen, Big Ben's task was to free Jan. I was going for Jane, and each of us was going to do as much damage as possible so we stood some chance of escape.

Amanda was going to do what she could with the nail guns – their effective range was only about ten metres, and then she was going to call the police. We needed them here to make the arrests and take the Sandman and his men away. Once the captives were safely ours, there was no reason not to involve Quinn.

Just about to swing the pickaxe handle I'd chosen as my weapon for this fight, I was thrown completely by lights filling the air and a voice barking commands over a loudspeaker.

'You are all under arrest! Lay down your weapons now, or I will give the order to open fire!'

The Sandman

I didn't need Amanda to call the police. They were already here!

The voice being amplified by the loudspeaker needed no introduction; I knew Ian Quinn's voice when I heard it. It came from my right, Quinn and his men emerging from the trees on a different flank to ours. They were moving fast, covering ground in a burst of movement the same way we were. How had they got here so fast? How had they got here at all?

Distracted by this unexpected ambush to my ambush, I missed my target – a man in a monk's robe who was coming to intercept me – and tripped over a root or something poking from the dirt.

Jane was six feet away from me as I sprawled on the ground, but she was at the back of the line of people and nearest the house.

When we concocted our hasty ambush plan, we had no idea who might emerge in what order or even when they would leave the house. It was just bad luck that I got to aim my efforts at the one who was farthest from us.

The men holding Jane ducked back into the house, dragging her with them and from my vantage point low on the ground, I had to watch the Sandman and his wife escape inside too. At least one other acolyte got inside and then the door slammed shut.

It was the hostage situation I had been trying so hard to avoid.

Cursing Chief Inspector Quinn, I grunted my determination, thrust off the ground and started running.

The Final Fight

SATURDAY, DECEMBER 24TH 1640HRS

Jane

The upwelling of emotion when I first heard, and then saw, Tempest was a level of euphoria I worried I might never match.

Lost, defeated, and ready to die one moment. Jubilant, excited, and ready to fight the next. I was only just outside the front door of the house when I heard his voice come over the radio and at that point still looking for a way to get near to the Sandman.

The knife was in my hand and ready to go. No one had seen it. If I could get close, I would just lunge and stab. If they kept me away from him, I would first stab the two men holding me and then run at the one I wanted to kill.

Tempest's appearance changed that plan in an instant. Suddenly I was imbued with a belief that we might win the day.

How many people had Tempest brought with him?

The Sandman

However many it was, this was the best chance we were going to get.

Terrifying roars came from all over the place, dark figures rushing the Sandman's acolytes. I twisted the knife around, bringing it out from its hiding place. I was going to stab the men holding me and anyone else I could get to. Anything I could do to help had to be the right thing to do.

Before I could do anything of the sort, a rough yank on my right arm pulled me off balance and the knife went flying away into the dark. The men holding me were running back to the house, hauling me along behind them. My feet were no longer under me and I could do nothing to arrest my motion.

Then the craziest thing happened. Lights came on in the woods.

Bright lights from torches so powerful it was painful to look at created shadows and silhouettes and a voice filled the night air.

I needed only a heartbeat to work out what I was hearing. The police were here – Tempest brought them with him!

Yet I was being dragged back inside the house, and no one could get to me before they would have me inside.

I saw Tempest lose his footing and fall right in front of me. To his right, my left as I looked out, Big Ben had already grabbed Jan. Joy swept through me seeing his rescue.

I got a final look at Tempest's face before the door slammed shut once more.

The Sandman was gasping great lungfuls of air, his breathing out of control as if terror had gripped him.

The woman slapped his face. Hard.

The noise was loud like a gunshot in the quiet of the house. The Sandman reeled back, stunned by the blow.

'You miserable failure!' the woman screeched.

She might have had more to say but the sound of a window smashing and something landing in the house stole the words away.

The monks were looking around in confusion, waiting for orders though surely they realised there was no way out of this situation now.

'Quick, get her to the basement,' the woman snapped, her eyes flaring with anger when the men holding me failed to move instantly.

Jolted into motion, they scooped me from the floor, but I thrashed against them. The knife was gone, but I wasn't going back into that basement.

Throwing my weight against one then throwing my head backward as the other followed me, I caught him on the bridge of his nose with a reverse headbutt. There was no technique or finesse involved, this was adrenalin and lack of options.

The one I caught with my head fell away, clutching his face as blood exploded from his nose. The second one made a grab for me and was rewarded with a high kick to his midriff that took the wind from him.

Snarling like a caged animal, I went to spin around to face the next attack but found myself gripped tightly from behind before I could.

'For goodness sake,' growled the Sandman's wife, her mouth right next to my ear. 'It's just one little girl.'

'No, it isn't,' said Tempest, stepping into the hallway.

There was a cut to his head, a nasty one judging by the amount of blood coming down the side of his face.

He saw me looking and wafted a dismissive hand at his

wound. 'I should have maybe protected my head when I dove through the window.' Turning serious, he asked. 'Are you all right, Jane?'

In my girl voice I said. 'I will be. Do you think I should tell them the truth?'

'What truth?' demanded the woman holding me. She was as tall as me, and surprisingly strong in a lean, wiry kind of way. However, pound for pound, men are always stronger.

I planted my feet and switched to my normal voice. 'There's something important you don't know about me, sweetie.'

The woman gasped and her grip went slack. I drove backward off my feet jabbing my right elbow up and around. It would have been vastly easier without my hands tied together but the blow struck under her chin with enough force to send her crashing into the wall.

She struck it with her head, a whimper escaping her lips as she slid down the wall to slump on the floor.

'Valerie!' cried the Sandman, darting forward to rescue his wife with a panicked look on his face.

I stepped into his path, blocking his route. My breathing came heavy, but it was under control. To my left, Tempest was fighting the remaining acolytes and outside, the sound of the police putting down any last pockets of resistance filled me with the confidence I needed to finish the task.

'What did you do?' the Sandman raged, spittle dripping from his lips as his eyes bulged insanely. He wanted to get around me to reach his wife and I wasn't going to let him. I could let the police tackle him. If I opened the door, they would be on him in seconds, but I wanted to do this for myself.

Switching back to Jane voice, I showed him my teeth,

pulling back my top lip in a snarl when I said, 'I stopped a hideous monster.'

Madness filled his eyes. 'You're not worthy of my song, you freak.' He rushed me then, throwing himself at me bodily.

I'm not a fighter, and I had to weigh fifty pounds less than him. Good thing I'd picked up a large wooden ornament from a shelf then.

His lunge was uncontrolled and ill-thought presenting his head as an easy target. I brought the novelty carved owl upward in a two-handed swing that connected under his chin.

Honestly, I wanted it to last longer. There was a primal need in me to rain down blow after blow in a cathartic release of pent-up rage.

Yet the first blow felled him as surely as someone pressing the off switch.

I got to do that because Tempest beat the crap out of the remaining two acolytes before they could get to me. I'd done something heroic. I'd beaten the Sandman, and I felt a sense of relief that defied words.

When Tempest pulled me into his arms and hugged me, I burst into tears.

Grey Hair

SATURDAY, DECEMBER 24TH 1648HRS

Tempest

Emerging from the house, we found ourselves surrounded by armed police. Mercifully, they recognised us for what we were and treated us as gently as they could when they dragged us to the side so they could swarm into the building.

The scene in front of the house was one of relatively organised chaos. There were police everywhere and the noise from a helicopter high above was causing them to have to shout to be heard. The Sandman's followers in the black robes had been rounded up and were in cuffs. Medics were attempting to resuscitate someone – it looked like another of the monks – but I was looking only for my friends and the other freed captives.

Amanda spotted me and called out. Waving and shouting until she was sure she had my attention, she barged her way through the press of people to get to me.

'Oh, goodness, Tempest, you're bleeding,' she gasped on seeing my face up close.

'It's just a small cut on my scalp.' Actually, I didn't know how big it was and figured it might need stitches to close it. 'Is everyone okay?' I asked the only question I wanted an answer to.

'We're all fine,' Amanda sobbed, a happy and relieved tear running down her cheek as she pulled Jane into a hug.

Jan arrived then, embracing Jane, and staying that way as Amanda took my arm and we wandered away.

Big Ben emerged from the dark with a monk's robe over his left arm.

'Is there a naked monk around here somewhere?' I asked, unsure what was going on.

Amanda sniggered.

Big Ben adjusted his arms, producing a pair of underpants. With a grin he said, 'Yup. I found Smiler and thought he might enjoy a little natural time.'

Shaking my head, I said, 'Ben you are so weird.'

It was a moment of joviality at the end of a day that had been filled with awfulness and fear.

'Weird?' he scoffed. 'I think you mean gorgeous, brave, and back in the game.'

'What are you talking about?' Amanda asked.

Big Ben flicked his head to make his hair shimmy in the night sky. It was like watching a commercial.

'I figured out why I kept striking out today,' he claimed, looking around for something. When his eyes stopped roving, he said, 'Ah, she'll do.'

Amanda growled grumpily. 'Ben, you've been striking out because women don't like being shagged and never called again. Trust me on this. We had a meeting; you're not getting any more action. Ever.'

He shot her a grin and waved his arm to attract a member of the tactical unit.

'I've been striking out,' he announced, 'Because I had a grey hair. I used my phone to take a video of my strikingly beautiful face and spotted it at the front of my hair line.'

I couldn't stop myself from laughing at him. 'Ben a single grey hair is not going to have any effect on whether a woman finds a man attractive.'

'Oh, yeah? Well, watch this. I had a grey hair and I've been striking out all day. I've plucked the grey hair …' the cop in the tactical unit uniform arrived and we got to see that beneath the helmet and armour it was a woman.

She unclipped her chinstrap and removed the helmet, shaking out her hair which fell in lustrous locks, cascading over her shoulders to frame olive skin and full, pouting lips.

Ben said, 'Hey, babe, that was exciting. How about you and I go somewhere and get to know each other?'

Amanda and I were both silent, waiting for her to slap his face or make a disgusted noise and wander off.

She grabbed his sleeve and dragged him away.

Amanda's jaw dropped open. I nudged it shut again with a gentle finger and held her to me.

Doing Something I Probably Shouldn't

SATURDAY, DECEMBER 24TH 1715HRS

Tempest

Big Ben caught up with us as we were wandering back down toward the carpark. We had to pass the bunker to get there and saw the police bringing out the Sandman's men. I didn't know if we had them all or not, I figured the police would work that out, but I wasn't going to put any thought to it now.

'Feeling better?' I asked my oversized friend.

'Much better, thank you.'

Amanda made a disgusted noise but kept her comments to herself.

Basic was playing his *Gameboy*.

Getting closer to the carpark that led into the park, I could see lights ahead. To start with, I figured it had to be a mobile headquarters set up to manage the incident but when we came through the last of the trees, I could see news vans.

Quinn, it turned out was already holding a press

conference. Unwilling to risk the press being able to discover the truth, he was giving them his version of events as swiftly as he could. They would run the headlines and have his story out in the morning. Serial killers were worthy of the national and international news. If a different version of events came out afterwards, it would be far too late for the press to change what had already been written.

They could print a retraction, yes, but would they? They would have a juicy story that sold copies of their paper or got folks to watch their channel.

Ahead of us was a large marquee, and inside it was a raised platform and several rows of chairs. Coming into the marquee, we were stopped by a pair of uniformed officers.

'We have orders to deny you entry, Mr Michaels,' one said.

Amanda leaned in to get his attention. 'Are you kidding me, Mark? Quinn is up there lying his butt off. You have to let Tempest in.'

Mark shook his head and did not look likely to be swayed. 'The chief inspector would have my job.'

Amanda was going to argue, but I touched her arm. 'Let's just watch from here for a moment, shall we?' I made it sound like we were going to behave, but I didn't move away, even though that was what the cops wanted me to do.

Watching the press conference and looking around the marquee, I was impressed at how quickly it had all been arranged. There were several senior-looking police officers in front of the lines of press where they sat on a raised platform looking down.

How apt for the chief inspector to want to look down at people.

'Who is that?' I asked, my question aimed at Amanda. I

was pointing my arm so she would know who I was talking about.

'That's the chief constable for Kent,' she told me.

Not only had Quinn been able to assemble all this in a record time, but he was able to gather his bosses to the scene to impress them as well. He had to have called them in advance and had them primed ...

'He knew this was happening.' I voiced my thoughts for my friends to hear. 'They got here so quickly.' Spinning around to face Amanda, Big Ben, Jane, Jan, and Basic, I let my thoughts spill words from my mouth. 'Think about it. How did he know where to send the cavalry? How long was it between parking Jagjit's car and arriving at the house? Thirty minutes? Less? It couldn't be much more than that and that's not long enough to get people anywhere.'

'He was following us,' Amanda concluded, probably remembering some of his tricks from when she worked under his command.

I listened to him for a few seconds. That Quinn would give us no credit was a foregone conclusion, but he had the nerve to sell our discoveries as his own.

Quinn hadn't seen me yet; we were in the dark just outside the marquee. 'What I can tell you for sure is that his reign of terror is over. We have apprehended thirty-three suspects, all of whom are involved in the murder of an as yet unconfirmed number of women over a thirty-year period.'

'How many women, Chief Inspector?' called a man's voice.

Quinn bowed his head and looked distraught for a moment. He was lapping up the attention before giving his answer. 'As I said, we cannot yet release the number, but it is believed to be more than twenty. It started with his wife who I believe he murdered in the early eighties.'

'No, he didn't.' I shouted loud enough to be heard.

The crowd of reporters swung their attention my way.

I was about to confront Quinn, and I had a pretty good idea for how it was going to go.

A murmur from the press, quickly became a buzz as word spread. They had recognised me and wanted to know what I was doing here.

Quinn chose to ignore my outburst and was attempting to continue with what he had been saying. The press were no longer listening though. They were asking me questions instead.

They were yet to leave their seats and come my way, but their cameras were pointing at me now and I could see one or two starting to get to their feet.

Smiling at Mark, the cop who didn't want to let me in, I said, 'You can let me pass, or I can take your boss's press with me. It's your choice, big fella.'

He wasn't going to give me an answer or make a decision, and I was going in regardless. Before setting off, I turned inward to Amanda and placed a kiss on her lips.

'I've been struggling to know what to get you for Christmas. I finally worked it out.' From my pocket I produced the keys for the Lotus. 'I didn't get a chance to gift wrap it, sorry. And it's stuck in the police impound. When you get it though, it's yours.' I kissed her again and hustled away to do what I probably should have done a long time ago.

The press had been throwing questions at me ever since I called Ian Quinn a liar and I had ignored them while I talked to Amanda.

Now it was time to address them. 'Ramsey Mitchell, or

the Sandman as Chief Inspector Quinn wants you to call him, is not the serial killer behind the murders.'

My statement caused an explosion of questions.

Standing just behind Quinn, the chief constable twitched as if given an electric shock. He tapped Quinn on the arm and whispered something only the two of them could hear.

Quinn's cheeks coloured but his hate-filled eyes never lost contact with mine.

The questions from the press kept coming but I never once looked the reporters' way. My blood was boiling and there was only one possible way this could end now.

Striding forward, all sense left far behind me, I raised an accusing finger at Chief Inspector Quinn.

'You put me in a cell. You put my whole team in cells last night and you did it at the risk of two people's lives.'

Quinn scoffed, 'You broke into a house.'

My voice got even louder. 'I broke into the house of a serial killer you refused to investigate!'

The tone of the reporters' questions changed. They wanted to know more about my claims.

'You endangered lives and broke into my office so you could steal the research my team had worked on to catch a man you denied could even exist. We were scrambling to avert a murder, and you hampered us at every turn because you couldn't stand to see me solve the case first.'

'The apprehension of criminals is the job of the police, Mr Michaels. You insist on breaking the law and jeopardising police investigations with your cowboy attitude and haphazard techniques.'

'You insist on claiming victory for the battles others have won. You didn't solve this case, Ian. Remember when I said you would wish you had chosen to do the right thing? Well, this is where that starts. There will be an investigation after tonight, the press will insist upon it. The greatest credit for solving this case and exposing the Sandman goes to Jane Butterworth.' I pointed to the marquee's entrance. 'Take a bow, Jane.' She waved and looked embarrassed. Turning back to face Quinn again, I chuckled at him. 'You lack the common decency most humans possess. Why don't you take this opportunity to thank Jane for her involvement?'

Quinn shuffled his notes and attempted to ignore my suggestion. 'I think we should get back to the meat of this press conference.'

He was instantly bombarded by questions about the Blue Moon team's involvement. I waited until someone asked the question I hoped to hear.

'Who is Jane Butterworth, Chief Inspector?'

I pounced. 'Yes, Chief Inspector. Who indeed? Will you address her as Jane?'

'No, I will not!' he snapped. 'He is a man in a woman's dress.'

I nodded my head. 'Well done, Chief Inspector. You just attacked the entire LGBTQ community live on television. That should put the brakes on your career.'

Quinn forced out a raucous guffaw, tipping his head back to let his laughter fill the air. When it rocked back to level, I punched him in the mouth.

A startled gasp rippled around the open area and everyone stopped moving.

Quinn dropped like a stone.

Standing in my eyeline now was the chief constable. He looked shocked.

I growled, 'Put your dog back on its leash.'

I was going to jail, that much was for certain now. It wouldn't matter what I had done in the past or how deserving Quinn was of it; you can't punch a policeman on television and not face consequences for your actions.

I was okay about it and was happy for the trade. Ian Quinn needed to be punched, and I believed punching him was the final guarantor I needed for them to actually launch an enquiry. He'd done almost nothing to solve this case while putting lives at risk with his ambition and I wanted someone to know.

Cops were rushing to get to me, or to get to the chief inspector who hadn't twitched since I decked him. I didn't resist when they ordered me to place my hands behind my back.

Amanda fought her way to me, using the fact that she knew all the cops to make them let her through. Though none of them said it, I think most of them wanted to give me a pat on the back for knocking their boss out, and one or two of them gave me a wink when the chief constable wasn't looking.

'Oh, Tempest,' sighed Amanda. 'What did you do?'

I gave her a lopsided, apologetic grin. 'What I had to do, babe. Can you look after the dogs for me, please? I guess I'll be out tomorrow sometime but back in court soon enough.'

She sighed again. 'They'll give you a month at least, regardless of the circumstances. You just did that on live TV. Letting you off would send a terrible message.'

I shrugged. 'I'll miss you when I am inside. I'll miss you tonight.'

She leaned in to kiss me. 'I'll have the turkey waiting for you.'

Feeling the gaze of the chief constable on them, the officers waiting to take me insisted Amanda step back, and they led me away.

The press conference was a disaster, but only for the police. The press loved it and chased the cops holding me all the way to the squad car they put me in.

In the back of the police car, I allowed myself to relax. It had been a frantic few days filled with worry, adrenalin-fuelled chases, too little sleep, and missed meals. Tonight, I would sleep like a baby, and charged with assault, I would be released in the morning until my court hearing. However far away that proved to be.

As things were, I couldn't come up with anything much to feel sad about.

Afterword

Hello, reader,

It is the Saturday between Good Friday and Easter Sunday as I write this final note. I finished the book in the small hours of this morning, staying up to crank out the last chapters because I was in a flow at that point.

I'm not entirely sure my wife approved of me sliding into bed at 0224hrs, but it's not like I was just getting in from the pub. She was good enough to leave me there to get an extra half an hour this morning, so I awoke when our baby daughter, who turns one this month, started poking me. She was tucked up next to me and had a smile for me when she discovered it was daddy and not mummy keeping her company.

This turned out to be the hardest book I have written since *Damaged but Powerful* about twelve months ago. On both occasions, it is the timeline that has thrown me. Most of my books I write chronologically from start to finish, the story flowing from my brain to the page in a flurry of fingers.

With *The Sandman*, I had already written *The Ghoul of Christmas Past* which overlaps the events in this story and thus created limitations on what I could write. I had not considered this until I sat down to write this book.

It was a bit of fiddle, and I kept trying to work out how to fit Patience into the story even though she was involved in events in the overlapping timeline. I am happy with the end result and hope you are too.

The dedication for this book is to a person in my author's Facebook group. He came up with the camouflage jackets as Basic's next endeavour and deserves the credit for his imagination. You can join the Facebook group too if you wish to, there is a link on the last page of this book. It's a cool place to exchange questions and thoughts about my books and you can find information there that is not available anywhere else.

I mention etorphine in this book. It is a semi-synthetic opioid possessing an analgesic potency approximately 1,000–3,000 times that of morphine. It was first prepared in 1960 from oripavine, which does not generally occur in opium poppy extract but rather the related plants Papaver orientale and Papaver bracteatum. Interestingly, it is the drug used by the serial killer anti-hero in the TV show Dexter. Its effects as an incapacitant are instant.

The second world war bunker in Cobham Woods is a real thing, it just isn't in Cobham Woods. I shifted it a couple of miles, but it exists in real life, not just my imagination. I really did stumble upon it while walking my dogs one day many years ago. Kent is littered with forgotten Spitfire hangers and sea defences from a time the oldest generation can just about remember but will seem like ancient history to my kids.

I have the chaps employ t-shirt guns in the bunker but

then found several of my advanced copy readers had no idea what it is. They use them at sports events and the like to launch t-shirts (and probably other soft merchandise items) into the back rows. It's a wide tube with a compressed air can attached. The t-shirt is packed tightly into a pack so it is much like firing a bean bag gun only not so dangerous.

With this book ready for publication, I need to shift my attention to the short story that follows it. I will write that next, so it is ready for people to download by the time they are reading this. Then I have more cozy mystery fun with my *Felicity Philips Investigates* series. It's time for book two in that series and then I have a Patricia tale to write and then another Albert, but the Blue Moon crew will be back really soon, and you can see the next book on the following page.

Take care.
Steve Higgs

Next in the Blue Moon Investigations Series

vinci-books.com/jailhouse-golem

There's a monster roaming the prison's passageways at night and it's just taken a life.

Incarcerated for a crime he gladly committed, paranormal detective, Tempest Michaels, has been enjoying the peace and quiet. But all that is about to change… The legend of the jailhouse golem is more than two hundred years old and though it has been investigated in the past, no one has ever come close to solving the mystery. He won't get paid for this one, but there's something more valuable at stake… his life.

Turn the page for a free preview…

Jailhouse Golem: Chapter One

MAIDSTONE PRISON MINIMUM-SECURITY WING

Thursday, May 11th 1736hrs

Dinnertime came around again as it does every day, and I left my cell to make my way to the mess hall. That I think of it as a mess hall harks back to my Army days. I served for long enough that the names for some things might have stuck in my head and may be there forever.

I sat with other inmates, eating our meals while chatting amiably about this or that or nothing much at all.

In the minimum-security wing, the guard to inmate ratio was even less than I expected, but no one in here was going to misbehave. Most prisoners were serving short sentences and would be home with their families - or whatever they had – soon enough. They just had to keep their heads down and do their time.

The same applied to me, yet my case was a little different from most others. I had enemies inside the walls that housed us all. None were in with me, but the main exercise yard was a large square in the centre of the prop-

The Sandman

erty where the prison looped around to enclose it on all four sides. The prisoners, separated into different wings, would sometimes pass each other as one came out and the other went in. We were on different sides of a fence, but I got spotted on only my second day inside.

I knew the face but could not put a name to it. He knew me though, shouting my name to the accompaniment of violent threats until two prison officers tackled him. One was a huge man, bigger even than my old army buddy, Big Ben. Not so much in height, though I judged he was a shade taller than Big Ben's six feet and seven inches, but in girth.

Where Big Ben was lean hard muscle, the guard was carrying another hundred pounds which was half fat and half muscle. He looked like a professional rugby player. Or perhaps someone a professional rugby team might take great interest in. However, when the inmate resisted, near foaming at the mouth with his desire to kill me, the guard performed a move I had only ever seen on television.

It caused me to reassess his athletic ability and relabel him as a wrestler. Doubly so when he then put the inmate in a sleeper hold.

'Move along, Michaels.' The instruction came from a prison officer called Gomez. He was friendly, as all the guards in minimum security seemed to be, but they were still prison officers, and I was an inmate.

In many ways, I was here by choice. I knew the probable consequences when I publicly chose to punch a chief inspector in the mouth. I say publicly, but what I mean is I did it live on national television at a press conference. To explain why, I would choose to remind you how a pearl is formed – through constant irritation.

Chief Inspector Quinn was the piece of grit stuck inside

my shell, and the punch was my solution. So I was in jail, though to be honest, I was rather enjoying it.

Adjusting to the slow pace of life in prison didn't take me as long as I expected it to. I had eight weeks to serve; my penalty for putting Chief Inspector Quinn on his backside.

Apparently, he required some dentistry following my single punch, but my hope I might be able to plead I used minimal force fell on deaf ears. Yes, I only punched him once and thus could not have hit him any fewer times. However, I also knocked him out with that first punch and the judge believed it had been premeditated.

I didn't bother to argue; it had been.

They put me in the minimum-security wing of Maidstone Prison. When I get out, I can walk across the road to the bar there and wait for Big Ben, Amanda, and the others to come find me.

I get to read books, and I can use the internet for an hour a day. There was a well-stocked gym I was choosing to visit six days out of every seven and felt certain I was going to drop a few pounds and return home distinctly leaner than I was when I arrived.

Even the food was pretty good, and with the total absence of alcohol from my diet, I was allowing myself the indulgent French toast they served at breakfast each morning. It was the best I had ever eaten.

All in all, getting locked up was a positive experience so far.

I was missing my dogs though. Bull and Dozer were staying with my girlfriend/business partner, Amanda. She was running my paranormal investigation business along with a third detective, my former assistant, Jane Butterworth.

They were more than capable of handling anything that

The Sandman

came up in the short time I was stuck inside, and I gave it all very little thought.

In fact, the only thing that made me think of my work life outside of the jail was a rumour going around of strange occurrences at night.

It started a few weeks ago when a giant man-shaped apparition was seen in the maximum-security wing. I hadn't known about it when they locked me up, but the prison, like so many other old buildings in England, was supposedly haunted, if that is the right word in this case. The ... thing is a golem – a man made from clay and given instruction by its creator. It has been seen many times during the history of the prison and was credited with severely grisly deaths. That's if you are prepared to believe all that nonsense.

I knew basic supernatural lore and legend – I couldn't really avoid picking up some knowledge in my job, but though I was mildly curious about what inmates might have seen, it was largely driven by the desire to debunk it.

When my head hit the pillow that night, I wasn't thinking about a golem though, I was thinking about rum. I wouldn't normally give rum, or alcohol of any kind, the slightest thought on a Thursday night. However, now cut off from the freedom to make choices for myself, I rather fancied a couple of beverages.

My idle fantasies didn't keep me awake for very long.

Jailhouse Golem: Chapter Two

RUDE AWAKENING

Friday, May 12th 0115hrs

'Michaels.'

The lights in my cell flicked on, bathing me in sudden light that was harsh on my eyes.

On the top bunk, Banksy swore loudly, questioning what might be happening.

I continued blinking, trying to force my eyes to adjust because something unusual was occurring and that was enough to put me on high alert.

I had enemies inside Maidstone Prison as I mentioned earlier. Plenty of them, in fact.

'Michaels, the warden wants you.' Squinting at the door as it swung open and a guard filled it, I could make out the rather tubby form of Officer Gomez.

I rubbed my face and swung my legs around. I'd only been in prison for a week; still settling in, one might say. The time on my watch showed 0115hrs.

The Sandman

Prison Officer Gomez delivered me to the Warden's office, why the man who ran the place was here so late at night only occurring to me to question as we reached his door.

Gomez knocked, waited to be invited in, and announced me.

I hadn't met the warden and never expected to. I was a minor offender in for a short period of time – there was nothing special about me.

So why did the warden want to see me in the middle of the night?

'You can go,' the warden dismissed his member of staff. Gomez closed the door on his way out.

It left just me and the warden in the room. He was looking at me, I was looking at him. He had trim grey hair and a close-cropped, yet full beard. His eyes were a silvery blue and gave the impression he was analysing me every bit as much as I was him. He wore a good suit, cut from a soft grey cloth, and his figure was trim. I guessed his age at mid-sixties and wondered how long he had to go until retirement.

Behind him on the desk, smoke twirled upward from a large cigar. I hated the smell of them and could feel the smoke tickling the back of my throat already. If I were anywhere else, I would complain or leave.

A second passed and I wondered if this was one of those daft power games where he was going to wait until I got bored or nervous and spoke only to then tell me he hadn't given me permission to speak. I just wanted to do my time, but though I had no desire to start acting like *Cool Hand Luke*, I wasn't going to be cowed into acting in a subservient manner.

It turned out I had him all wrong because in the next

heartbeat, he crossed the room with his right hand out and reaching for mine.

'Tempest Michaels,' he greeted me. 'I must say this is a real pleasure.'

'Is it?' I questioned, unsure as to what he might be referring. 'I'm in jail and it's the middle of the night.'

My response made him laugh, a big belly chuckle rumbling through him as he let my hand go again.

'I dare say the experience is rather different for you than for me. I have been a close follower of your work for a year now. Ever since that incident with Richard Claythorn. I read about it in the paper and was gripped. I always felt I missed my calling, you know. I should have pursued a career as a detective and put people behind bars, not made sure they reformed themselves once they were.'

'Warden I am curious to hear why I was summoned.' I hoped it wasn't just so he could meet me because I was getting a weird fanboy vibe. If he asked to take a selfie with me, I wasn't sure how I might react.

Scratch that. I knew exactly how I was going to react. I wanted a week off for each picture.

Unfortunately, that wasn't it.

He turned serious suddenly, everything from the timbre of his voice to the set of his face changed.

'I'm afraid I have need of your skills, Mr Michaels.' I hitched an eyebrow. 'Are you aware of the legend of the prison golem?'

I pulled the eyebrow back down. 'I am, but only in the vaguest manner,' I admitted.

The warden began to tell me a tale and while doing so, he backed away to a cabinet in the corner, from whence he then produced a crystal decanter and two glasses. Without asking, he poured two measures and lifted one for me to take.

I couldn't tell what it might be and was not in the habit of drinking neat spirits. However, I was also going to be completely teetotal for the duration of my stay so figured I might as well grab the chance to have a drop.

It would have been rude not to. That's what I told myself anyway.

A sniff told me it was brandy – not a spirit I would ever choose - but my attention was on the warden and his story. It went back to the early nineteenth century, making the legend over two hundred years old. A giant form attacked and killed three inmates on July eighth, 1809, tearing their limbs off inside their cells which were still locked when the guards arrived.

Other inmates described the creature having caught a glimpse of it as it passed by the small, barred window of their cell doors. The guards found unexplainable clay footprints leading into and back out of the prison. They terminated at one of the prison's external walls.

There were further incidents over the years, including four more deaths that were attributed to the golem. Each time, the deaths took place in C Wing, the maximum-security area, and on every occasion the footprints were discovered, and a hulking human form was reported.

'The last incident was in 1951,' the warden revealed.

I had a nasty feeling he was about to add something else to that statement.

'That should be the last incident used to be in 1951,' he continued, 'because we had a new one tonight.'

I said a few rude words inside my head.

Keeping the sigh I felt inside, I sought clarification. 'You want me to look into it, Warden, don't you?'

'Look into it?' The warden's eyes sparkled with excitement. 'No, man, I want you to catch it.'

Jailhouse Golem: Chapter Three

ME AND MY BIG MOUTH

Friday, May 12th 0129hrs

My opinion on the matter was of no interest to the warden who had a dead prison officer he was currently keeping quiet from everyone but those few who already knew.

I did, however, feel the need to voice my reservations.

'I must say the legend,' I chose my words carefully because I was sure it was all utter nonsense, 'sounds intriguing, but I am not in C Wing.'

The warden skewed his lips to one side.

'Hmm, yes, that does present a barrier, doesn't it?' He tracked back to his desk where he pressed a button to activate a personal address system. 'Superintendent Yardley to the warden's office, please.'

The door behind me opened mere seconds later, a tall, broad-shouldered man in a starched uniform striding through it with purpose.

'You summoned me, sir?' asked the man, clearly the prison superintendent. He was another man I was yet to meet but had heard the rumours and free advice never to cross the head guard. His tone, the way he addressed the warden, suggested he was not content to be summoned like a dog.

The warden looked beyond me to the man now crossing his office. 'I need you to transfer prisoner Michaels to C Wing, effective immediately.'

My eyebrows went for the sky. 'Whoa there, warden. I'm in minimum security. C Wing is maximum security.'

'It will only be for a short period,' the warden assured me dismissively.

I choked out a laugh though there was nothing amusing about his plan. 'I have … opponents in C Wing,' I pointed out tentatively. 'Quite a few of them.'

The number, I knew for a fact, was forty-three. For a year, I had been solving cases and seeing to it that I did so in such a way that the people responsible for the crimes I was called to investigate went to jail. There were fourteen former Klowns in C Wing for a start. All former criminals with time under their belt when I caught them, they had chosen to follow a man who brought a plague of terror to the county.

Then there were another dozen followers of the Sandman and the Sandman himself. They had only been in here for a few weeks which meant my face would be fresh in their minds. Add to that list some gangsters from Lithuania who I found beneath Chatham Dockyard - they were using the tunnels as a smuggling route, and you can see how the concept of moving to C Wing was making my pulse race.

I explained this to the warden. He was good enough to listen, but my concerns did nothing to sway his course.

To Superintendent Yardley, he said, 'Make sure he has a

suitable cellmate — someone who will be able to keep the others off his back.'

'Claude is without a cellmate, sir.'

The warden nodded with a smile. 'Perfect. Claude will do nicely.'

Claude, huh? Why was an alarm bell ringing in my head? 'Is there a reason why he has no cellmate?' I asked, even though I worried I might not like the answer.

Superintendent Yardley smiled at me. 'His last cellmate met with an unfortunate accident, Michaels.' He gestured with his head — time to go.

The warden was already back behind his desk, his attention on something else. As I got to the door, he called for the superintendent to wait.

'Michaels,' he addressed me. 'I do hope you can solve this thing swiftly. If C Wing is as hostile as you believe, you won't want to be in there for long.'

And there it was, a simple threat, subtly delivered. I was going into maximum security where a platoon of criminals I put away were serving hard time. How many of them would happily kill me if they got the chance?

All I had to do was solve a two-hundred-year-old mystery and catch the person behind a fresh murder.

Super.

Grab your copy...
vinci-books.com/jailhouse-golem